TEEN TITANS GO!™

SAVE THE DATE AND OPPOSITE DAY!

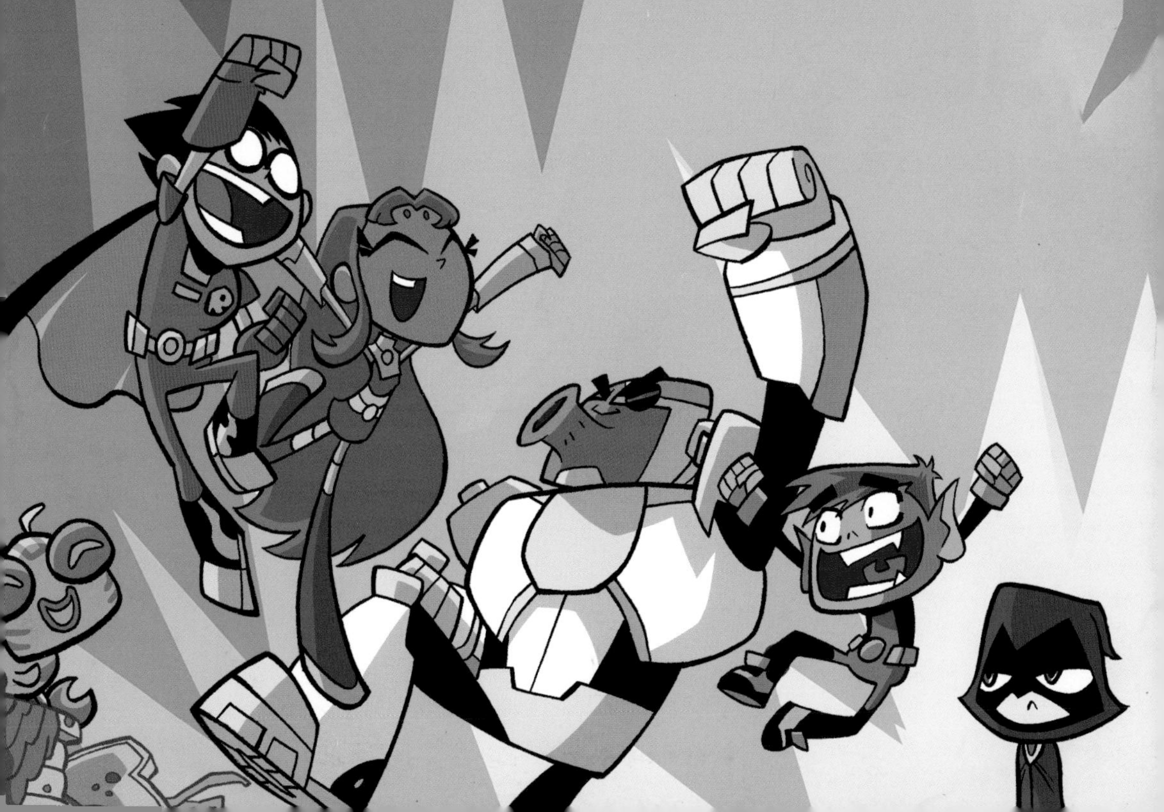

Teen Titans Go! is published by
Stone Arch Books, an imprint of Capstone.
1710 Roe Crest Drive
North Mankato, MN 56003
www.capstonepub.com

Library of Congress Cataloging-in-Publication Data is available at the Library of Congress website.
ISBN: 978-1-4965-9944-5 (library binding)
ISBN: 978-1-4965-9945-2 (eBook PDF)

Summary: Raven thought things couldn't get any worse after Starfire posted an online dating profile for
herself . . . until she posts one for Raven too. Then, it's "Opposite Day" at Titans Tower and chaos reigns
supreme! But you know what they say about Opposite Day: it's all fun and games until someone accidentally
tears open a rift into the Anti-Matter Universe.

Alex Antone, Editor – Original Series

STONE ARCH BOOKS
Eliza Leahy, Editor
Kyle Grenz, Designer
Hilary Wacholz, Art Director
Kathy McColley, Production Specialist

Printed and bound in the USA.
PA117

TEEN TITANS GO!

SHOLLY FISCH
WRITER

LEA HERNANDEZ DARIO BRIZUELA
ARTISTS

LEA HERNANDEZ JEREMY LAWSON
COLORISTS

WES ABBOTT
LETTERER

DAN HIPP
COVER ARTIST

STONE ARCH BOOKS
a capstone imprint

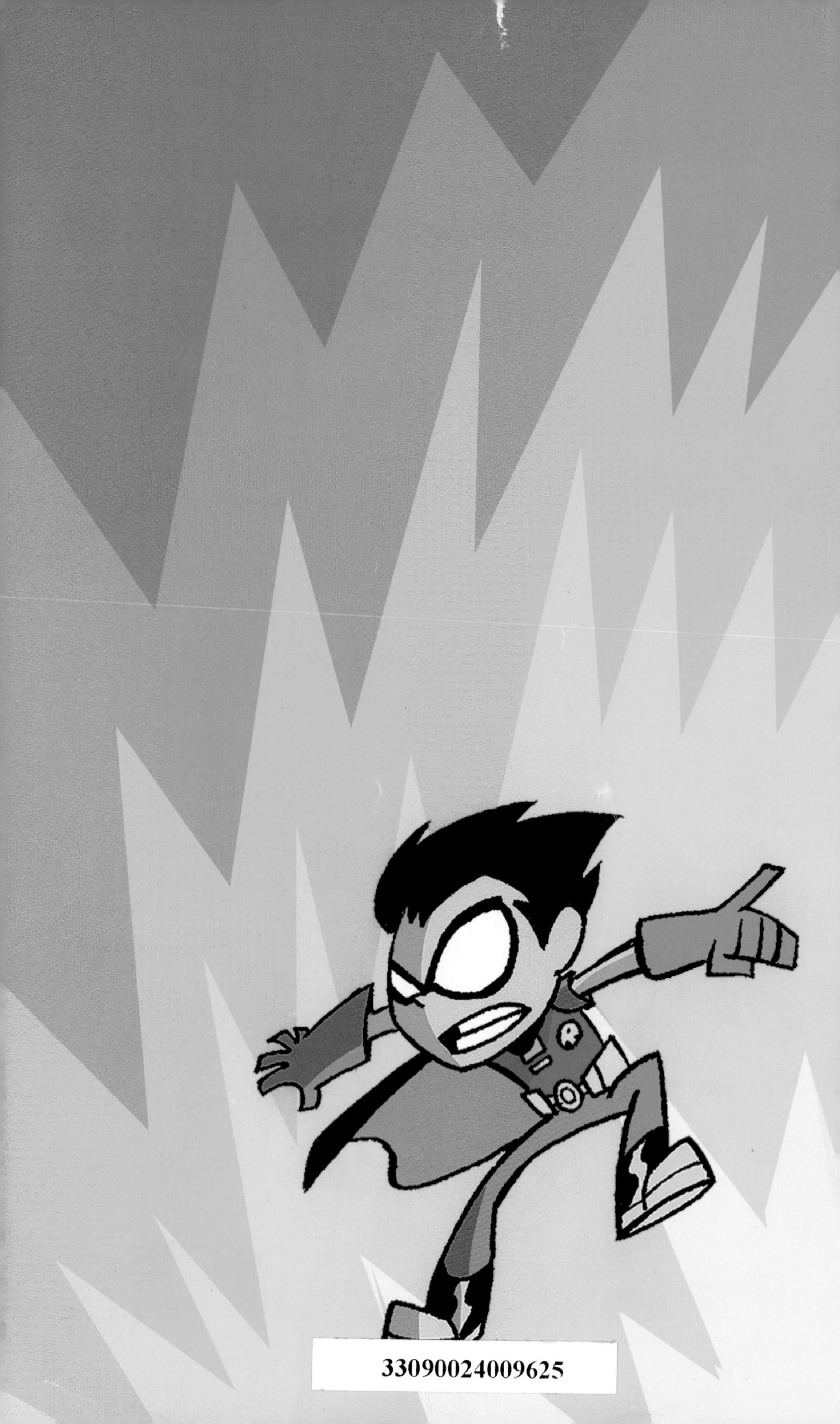

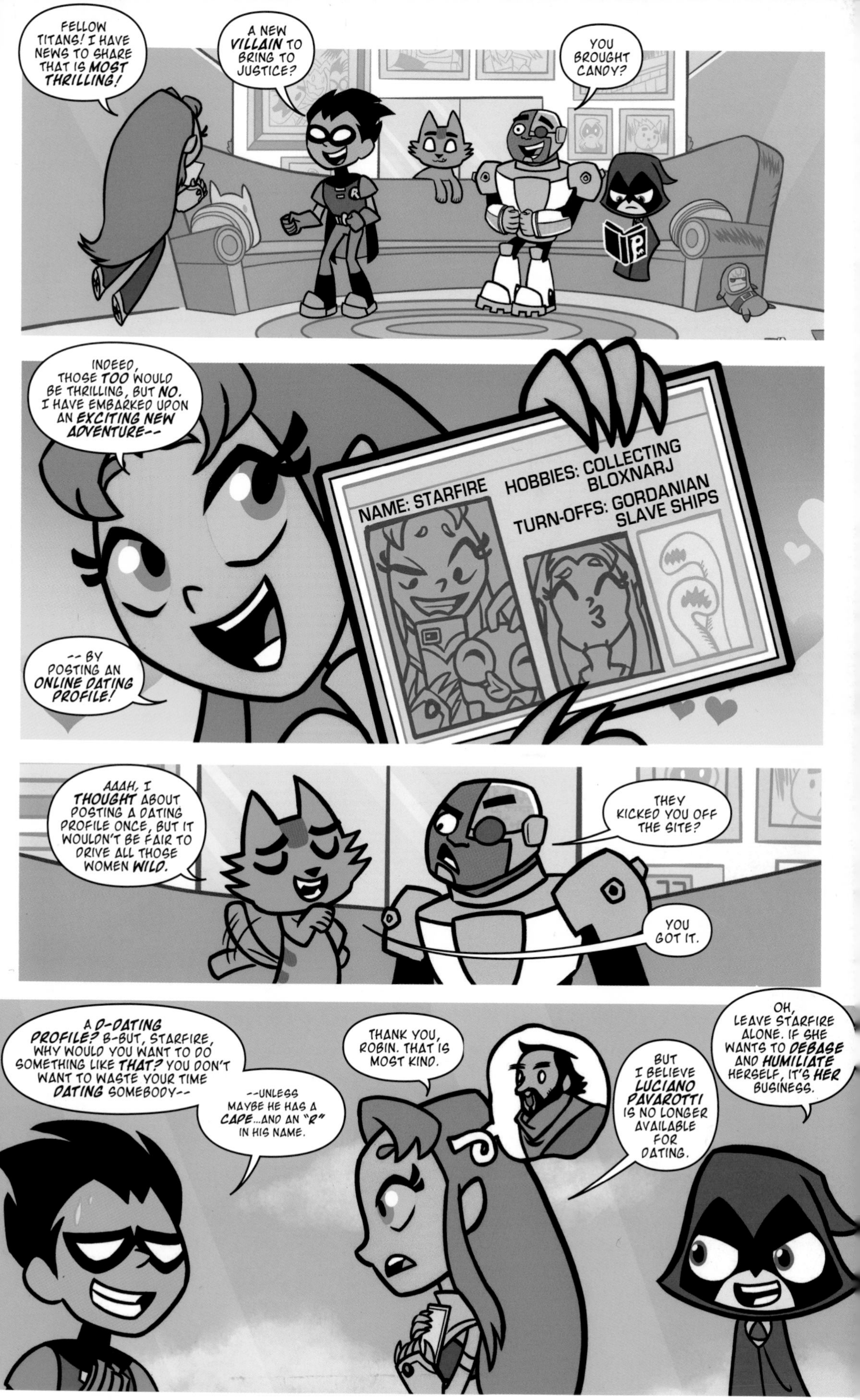
FELLOW TITANS! I HAVE NEWS TO SHARE THAT IS MOST THRILLING!
A NEW VILLAIN TO BRING TO JUSTICE?
YOU BROUGHT CANDY?
INDEED, THOSE TOO WOULD BE THRILLING, BUT NO. I HAVE EMBARKED UPON AN EXCITING NEW ADVENTURE--
NAME: STARFIRE
HOBBIES: COLLECTING BLOXNARJ
TURN-OFFS: GORDANIAN SLAVE SHIPS
-- BY POSTING AN ONLINE DATING PROFILE!
AAAH, I THOUGHT ABOUT POSTING A DATING PROFILE ONCE, BUT IT WOULDN'T BE FAIR TO DRIVE ALL THOSE WOMEN WILD.
THEY KICKED YOU OFF THE SITE?
YOU GOT IT.
A D-DATING PROFILE? B-BUT, STARFIRE, WHY WOULD YOU WANT TO DO SOMETHING LIKE THAT? YOU DON'T WANT TO WASTE YOUR TIME DATING SOMEBODY--
--UNLESS MAYBE HE HAS A CAPE...AND AN "R" IN HIS NAME.
THANK YOU, ROBIN. THAT IS MOST KIND.
BUT I BELIEVE LUCIANO PAVAROTTI IS NO LONGER AVAILABLE FOR DATING.
OH, LEAVE STARFIRE ALONE. IF SHE WANTS TO DEBASE AND HUMILIATE HERSELF, IT'S HER BUSINESS.

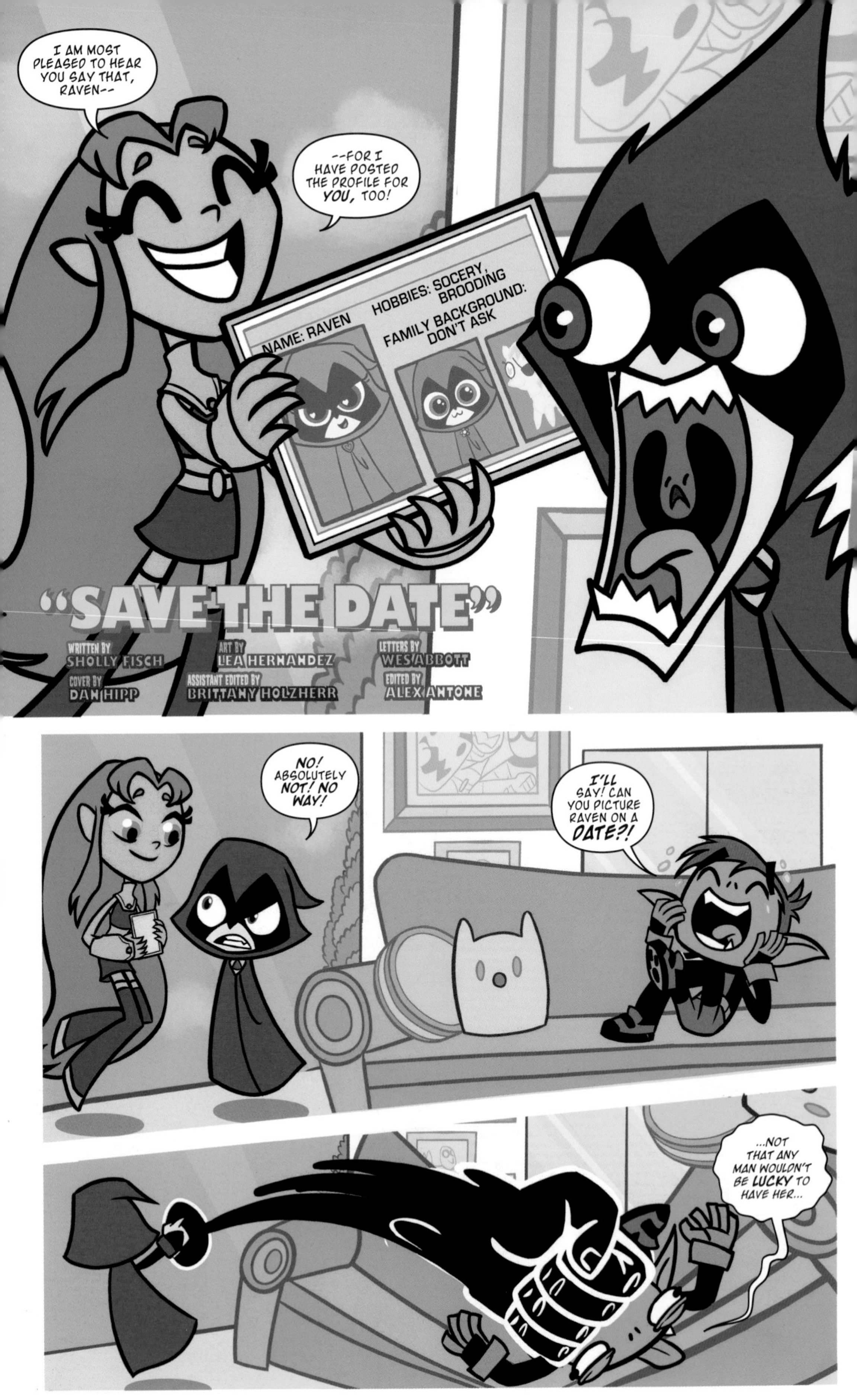

I AM MOST PLEASED TO HEAR YOU SAY THAT, RAVEN--
--FOR I HAVE POSTED THE PROFILE FOR YOU, TOO!
NAME: RAVEN
HOBBIES: SOCERY, BROODING
FAMILY BACKGROUND: DON'T ASK
"SAVE THE DATE"
WRITTEN BY SHOLLY FISCH
ART BY LEA HERNANDEZ
LETTERS BY WES ABBOTT
COVER BY DAN HIPP
ASSISTANT EDITED BY BRITTANY HOLZHERR
EDITED BY ALEX ANTONE
NO! ABSOLUTELY NOT! NO WAY!
I'LL SAY! CAN YOU PICTURE RAVEN ON A DATE?!
...NOT THAT ANY MAN WOULDN'T BE LUCKY TO HAVE HER...

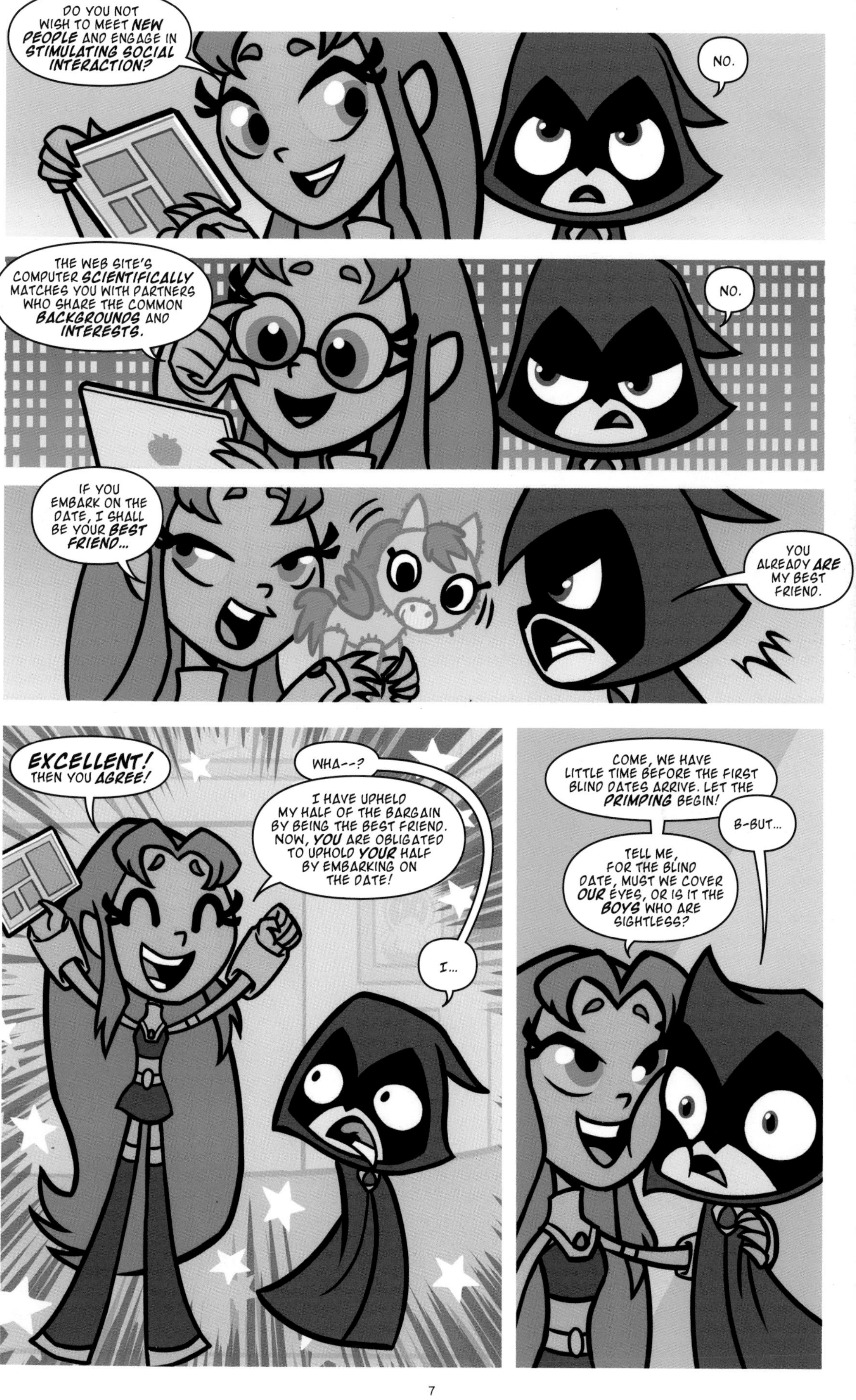
DO YOU NOT WISH TO MEET NEW PEOPLE AND ENGAGE IN STIMULATING SOCIAL INTERACTION?
NO.
THE WEB SITE'S COMPUTER SCIENTIFICALLY MATCHES YOU WITH PARTNERS WHO SHARE THE COMMON BACKGROUNDS AND INTERESTS.
NO.
IF YOU EMBARK ON THE DATE, I SHALL BE YOUR BEST FRIEND...
YOU ALREADY ARE MY BEST FRIEND.
EXCELLENT! THEN YOU AGREE!
WHA--?
I HAVE UPHELD MY HALF OF THE BARGAIN BY BEING THE BEST FRIEND. NOW, YOU ARE OBLIGATED TO UPHOLD YOUR HALF BY EMBARKING ON THE DATE!
I...
COME, WE HAVE LITTLE TIME BEFORE THE FIRST BLIND DATES ARRIVE. LET THE PRIMPING BEGIN!
B-BUT...
TELL ME, FOR THE BLIND DATE, MUST WE COVER OUR EYES, OR IS IT THE BOYS WHO ARE SIGHTLESS?

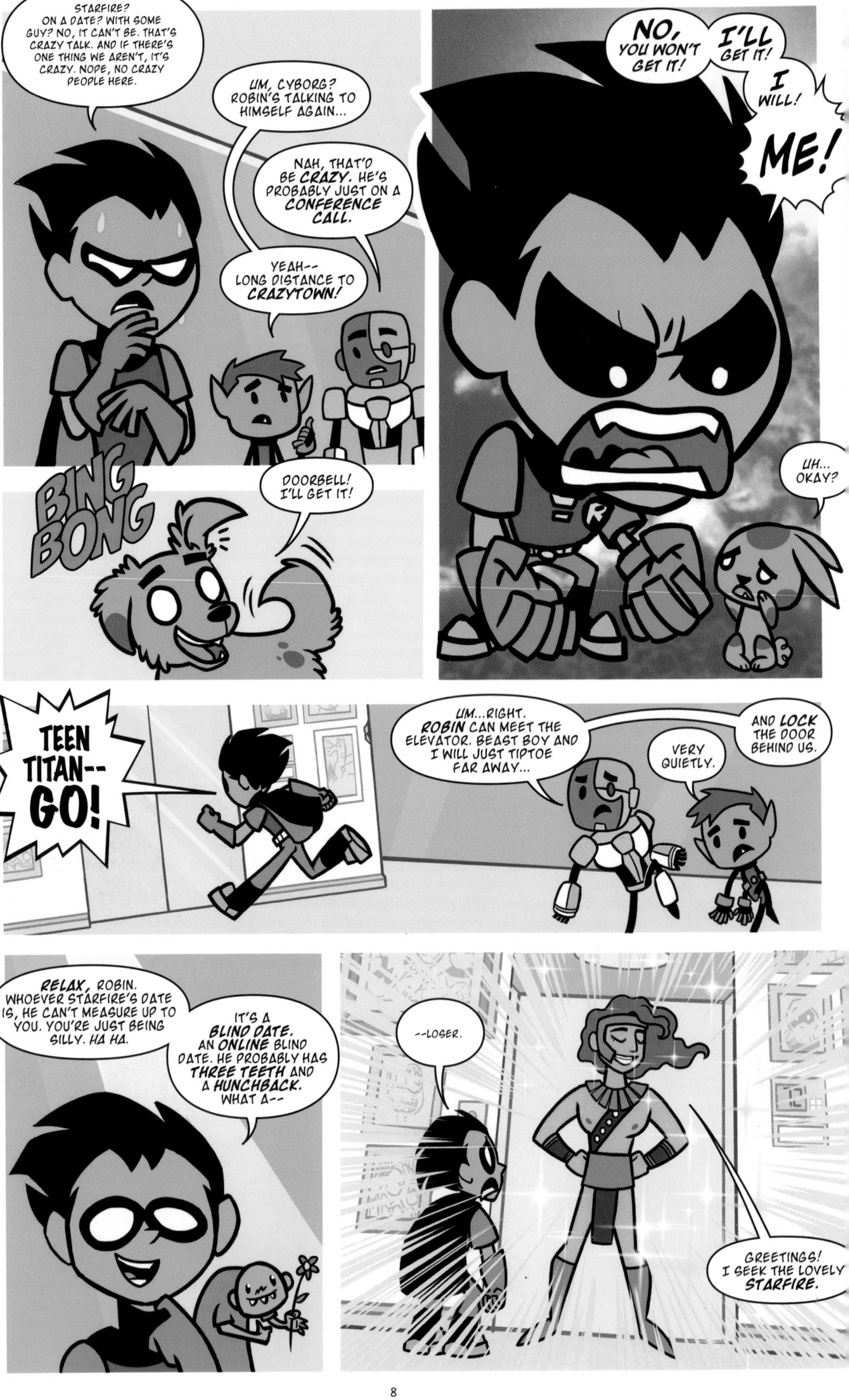
STARFIRE? ON A DATE? WITH SOME GUY? NO, IT CAN'T BE. THAT'S CRAZY TALK. AND IF THERE'S ONE THING WE AREN'T, IT'S CRAZY. NOPE, NO CRAZY PEOPLE HERE.
UM, CYBORG? ROBIN'S TALKING TO HIMSELF AGAIN...
NAH, THAT'D BE CRAZY. HE'S PROBABLY JUST ON A CONFERENCE CALL.
YEAH-- LONG DISTANCE TO CRAZYTOWN!
NO, YOU WON'T GET IT!
I'LL GET IT!
I WILL!
ME!
BING BONG
DOORBELL! I'LL GET IT!
UH... OKAY?
TEEN TITAN-- GO!
UM...RIGHT. ROBIN CAN MEET THE ELEVATOR. BEAST BOY AND I WILL JUST TIPTOE FAR AWAY...
VERY QUIETLY.
AND LOCK THE DOOR BEHIND US.
RELAX, ROBIN. WHOEVER STARFIRE'S DATE IS, HE CAN'T MEASURE UP TO YOU. YOU'RE JUST BEING SILLY. HA HA.
IT'S A BLIND DATE. AN ONLINE BLIND DATE. HE PROBABLY HAS THREE TEETH AND A HUNCHBACK. WHAT A--
--LOSER.
GREETINGS! I SEEK THE LOVELY STARFIRE.

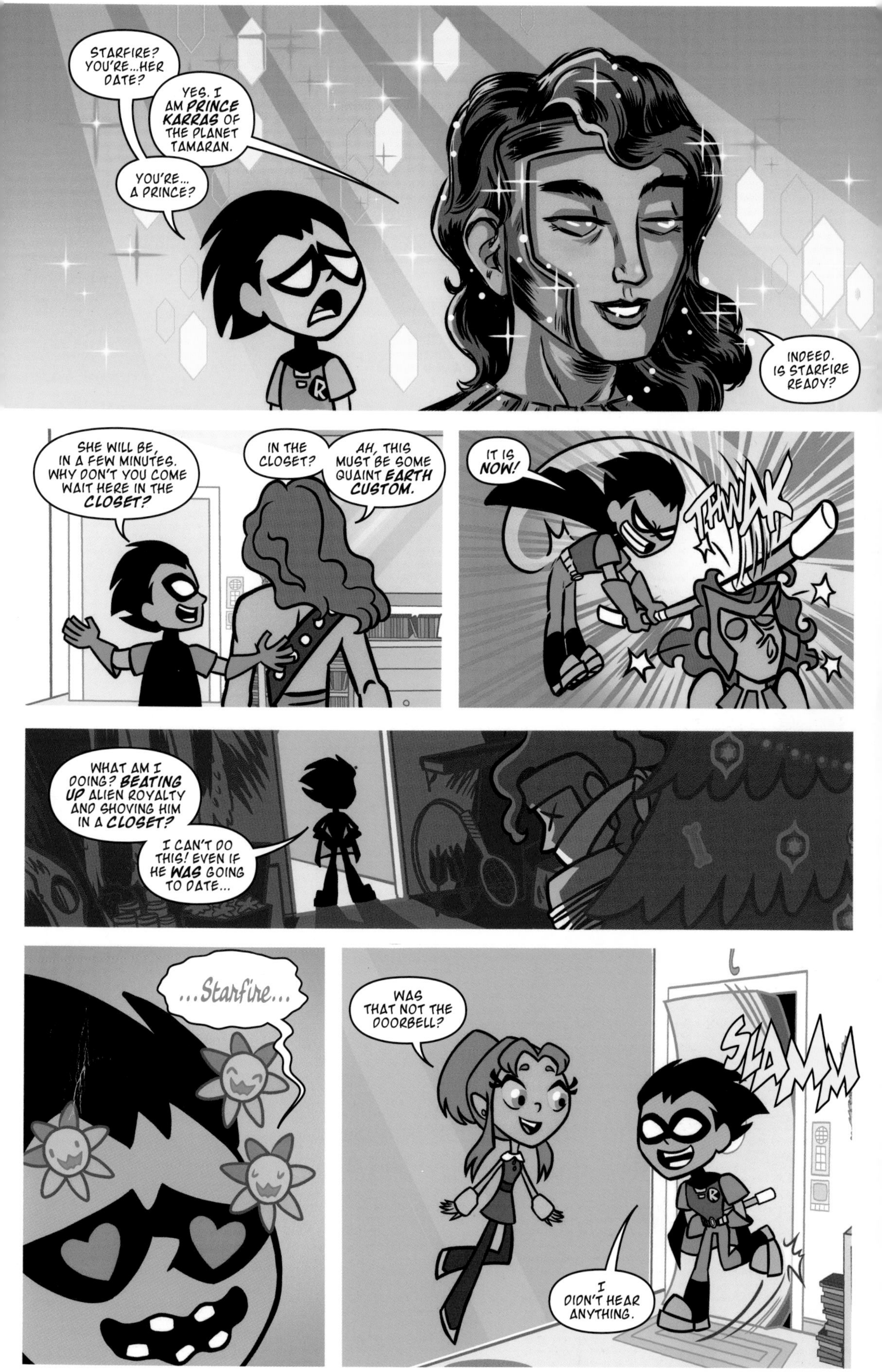
STARFIRE? YOU'RE...HER DATE?
YES. I AM PRINCE KARRAS OF THE PLANET TAMARAN.
YOU'RE... A PRINCE?
INDEED. IS STARFIRE READY?
SHE WILL BE, IN A FEW MINUTES. WHY DON'T YOU COME WAIT HERE IN THE CLOSET?
IN THE CLOSET?
AH, THIS MUST BE SOME QUAINT EARTH CUSTOM.
IT IS NOW!
THWAK
WHAT AM I DOING? BEATING UP ALIEN ROYALTY AND SHOVING HIM IN A CLOSET?
I CAN'T DO THIS! EVEN IF HE WAS GOING TO DATE...
...Starfire...
WAS THAT NOT THE DOORBELL?
SLAMM
I DIDN'T HEAR ANYTHING.

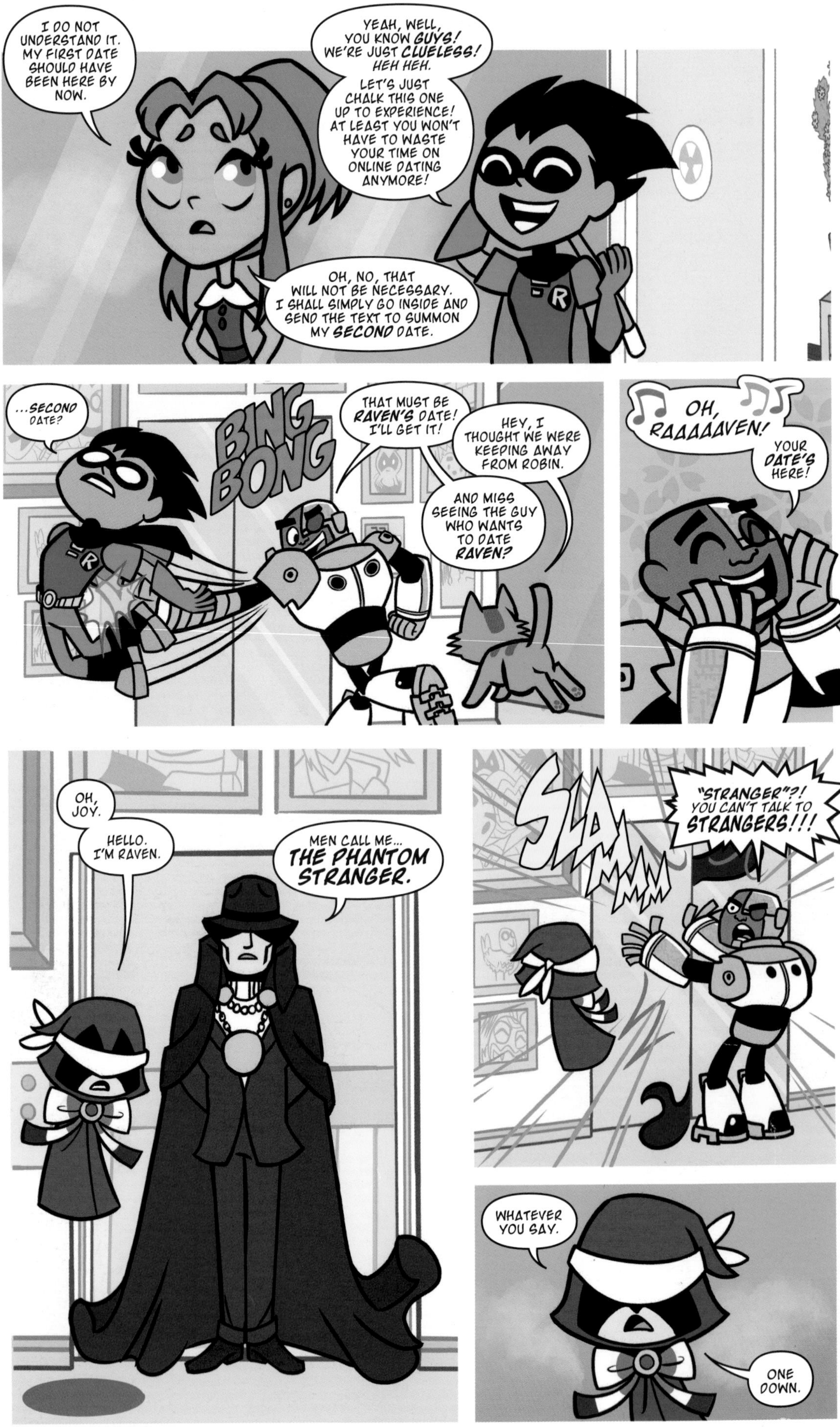

I DO NOT UNDERSTAND IT. MY FIRST DATE SHOULD HAVE BEEN HERE BY NOW.
YEAH, WELL, YOU KNOW GUYS! WE'RE JUST CLUELESS! HEH HEH.
LET'S JUST CHALK THIS ONE UP TO EXPERIENCE! AT LEAST YOU WON'T HAVE TO WASTE YOUR TIME ON ONLINE DATING ANYMORE!
OH, NO, THAT WILL NOT BE NECESSARY. I SHALL SIMPLY GO INSIDE AND SEND THE TEXT TO SUMMON MY SECOND DATE.
...SECOND DATE?
BING BONG
THAT MUST BE RAVEN'S DATE! I'LL GET IT!
HEY, I THOUGHT WE WERE KEEPING AWAY FROM ROBIN.
AND MISS SEEING THE GUY WHO WANTS TO DATE RAVEN?
OH, RAAAAAVEN!
YOUR DATE'S HERE!
OH, JOY.
HELLO. I'M RAVEN.
MEN CALL ME... THE PHANTOM STRANGER.
SLAMMM
"STRANGER"?! YOU CAN'T TALK TO STRANGERS!!!
WHATEVER YOU SAY.
ONE DOWN.

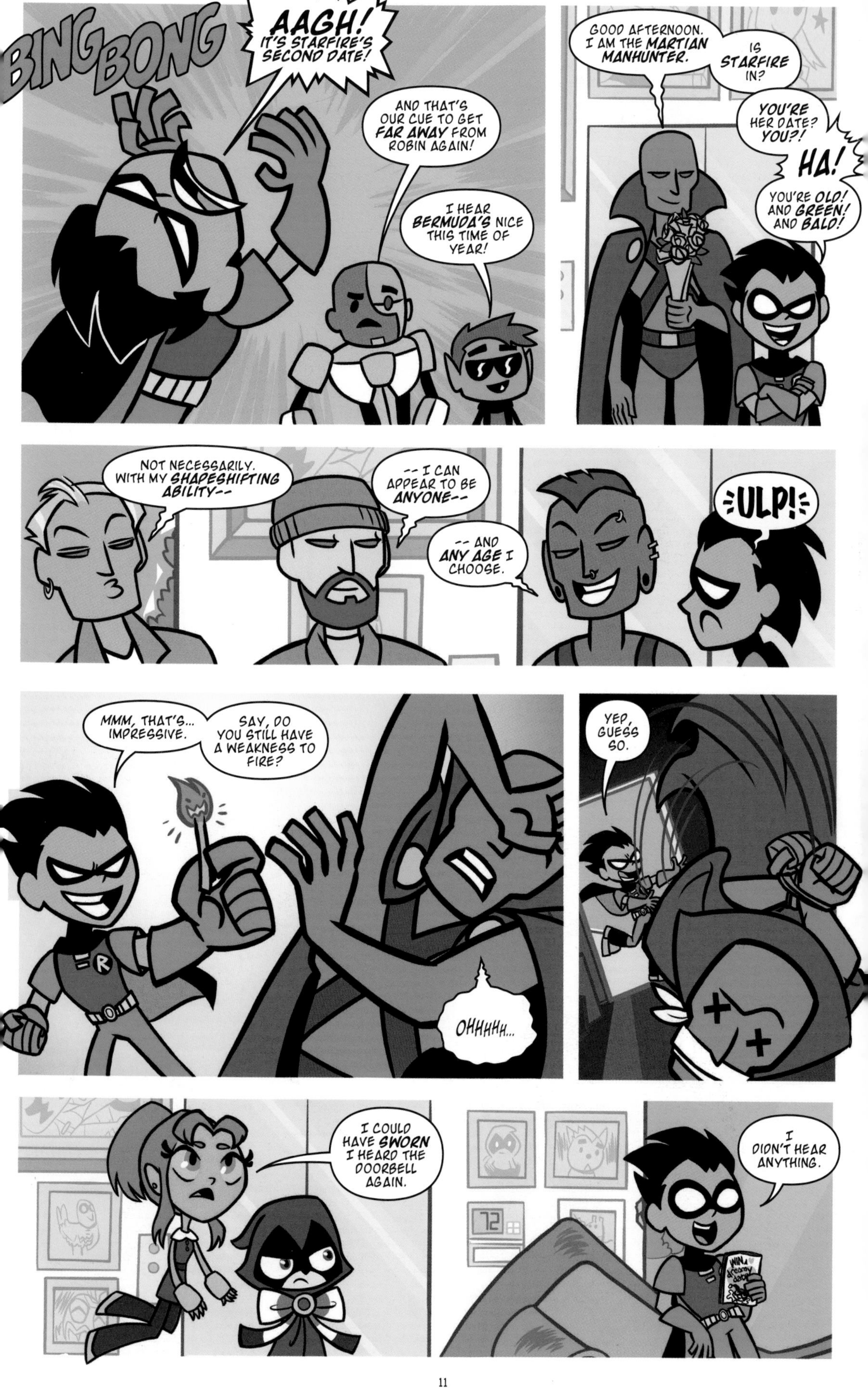
BING BONG
AAGH! IT'S STARFIRE'S SECOND DATE!
AND THAT'S OUR CUE TO GET FAR AWAY FROM ROBIN AGAIN!
I HEAR BERMUDA'S NICE THIS TIME OF YEAR!
GOOD AFTERNOON. I AM THE MARTIAN MANHUNTER.
IS STARFIRE IN?
YOU'RE HER DATE? YOU?!
HA!
YOU'RE OLD! AND GREEN! AND BALD!
NOT NECESSARILY. WITH MY SHAPESHIFTING ABILITY--
-- I CAN APPEAR TO BE ANYONE--
-- AND ANY AGE I CHOOSE.
ULP!
MMM, THAT'S... IMPRESSIVE.
SAY, DO YOU STILL HAVE A WEAKNESS TO FIRE?
OHHHHH...
YEP, GUESS SO.
I COULD HAVE SWORN I HEARD THE DOORBELL AGAIN.
I DIDN'T HEAR ANYTHING.

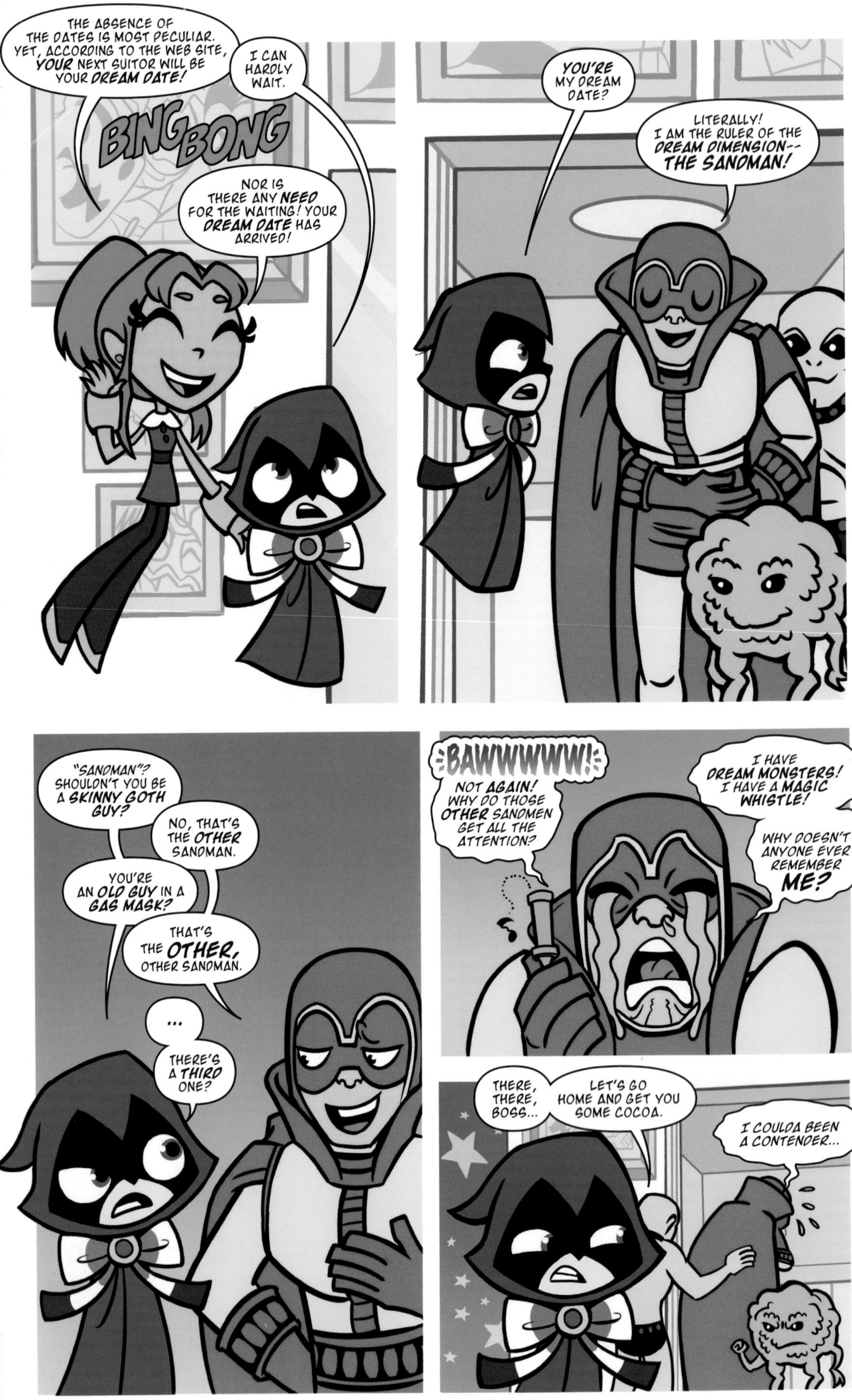
THE ABSENCE OF THE DATES IS MOST PECULIAR. YET, ACCORDING TO THE WEB SITE, YOUR NEXT SUITOR WILL BE YOUR DREAM DATE!
I CAN HARDLY WAIT.
BING BONG
NOR IS THERE ANY NEED FOR THE WAITING! YOUR DREAM DATE HAS ARRIVED!
YOU'RE MY DREAM DATE?
LITERALLY! I AM THE RULER OF THE DREAM DIMENSION-- THE SANDMAN!
"SANDMAN"? SHOULDN'T YOU BE A SKINNY GOTH GUY?
NO, THAT'S THE OTHER SANDMAN.
YOU'RE AN OLD GUY IN A GAS MASK?
THAT'S THE OTHER, OTHER SANDMAN.
...
THERE'S A THIRD ONE?
BAWWWWW!
NOT AGAIN! WHY DO THOSE OTHER SANDMEN GET ALL THE ATTENTION?
I HAVE DREAM MONSTERS! I HAVE A MAGIC WHISTLE!
WHY DOESN'T ANYONE EVER REMEMBER ME?
THERE, THERE, BOSS...
LET'S GO HOME AND GET YOU SOME COCOA.
I COULDA BEEN A CONTENDER...

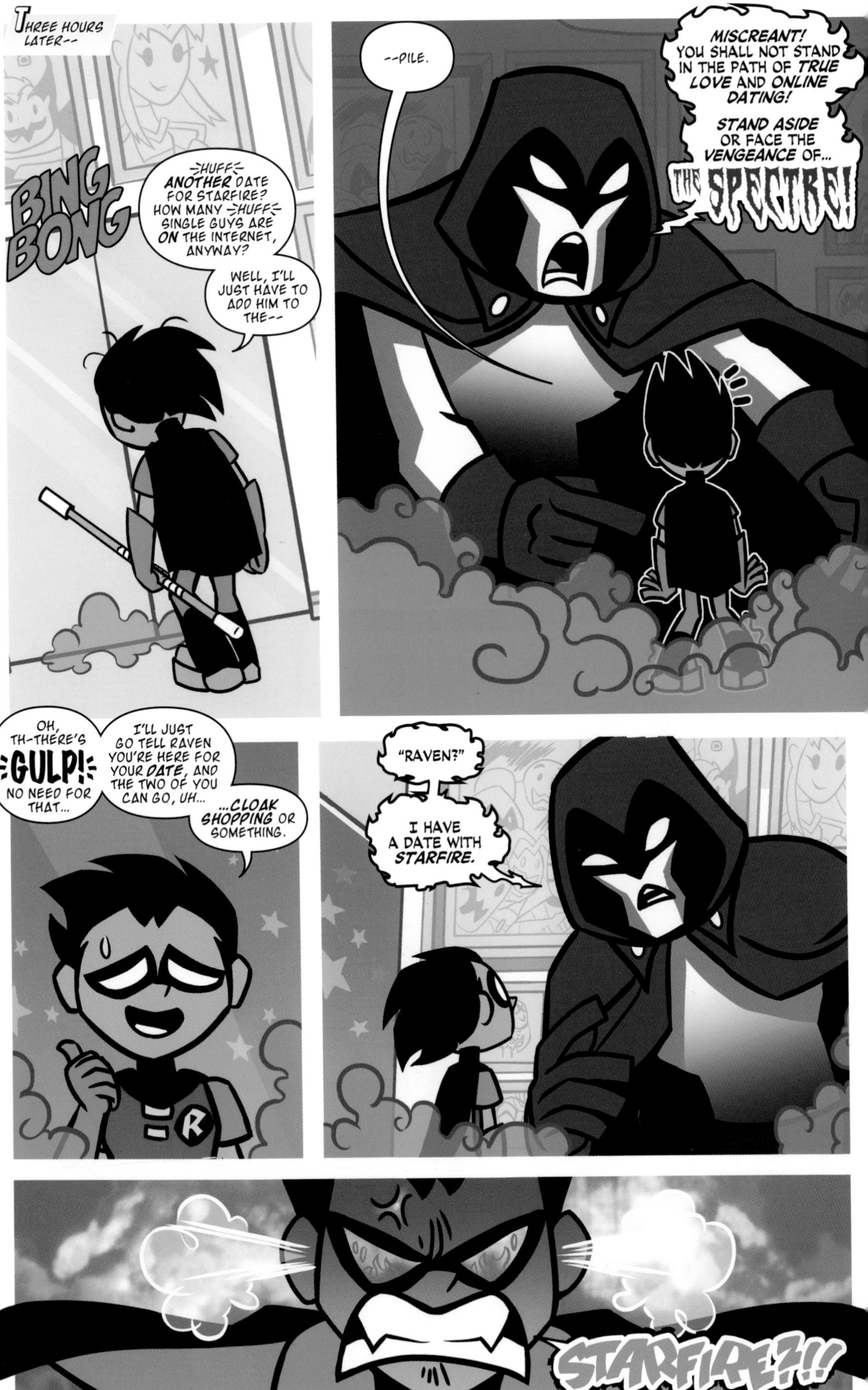
Three hours later--
BING BONG
=HUFF= ANOTHER DATE FOR STARFIRE? HOW MANY =HUFF= SINGLE GUYS ARE ON THE INTERNET, ANYWAY?
WELL, I'LL JUST HAVE TO ADD HIM TO THE--
--PILE.
MISCREANT! YOU SHALL NOT STAND IN THE PATH OF TRUE LOVE AND ONLINE DATING!
STAND ASIDE OR FACE THE VENGEANCE OF... THE SPECTRE!
OH, TH-THERE'S =GULP!= NO NEED FOR THAT...
I'LL JUST GO TELL RAVEN YOU'RE HERE FOR YOUR DATE, AND THE TWO OF YOU CAN GO, UH...
...CLOAK SHOPPING OR SOMETHING.
"RAVEN?"
I HAVE A DATE WITH STARFIRE.
STARFIRE?!!

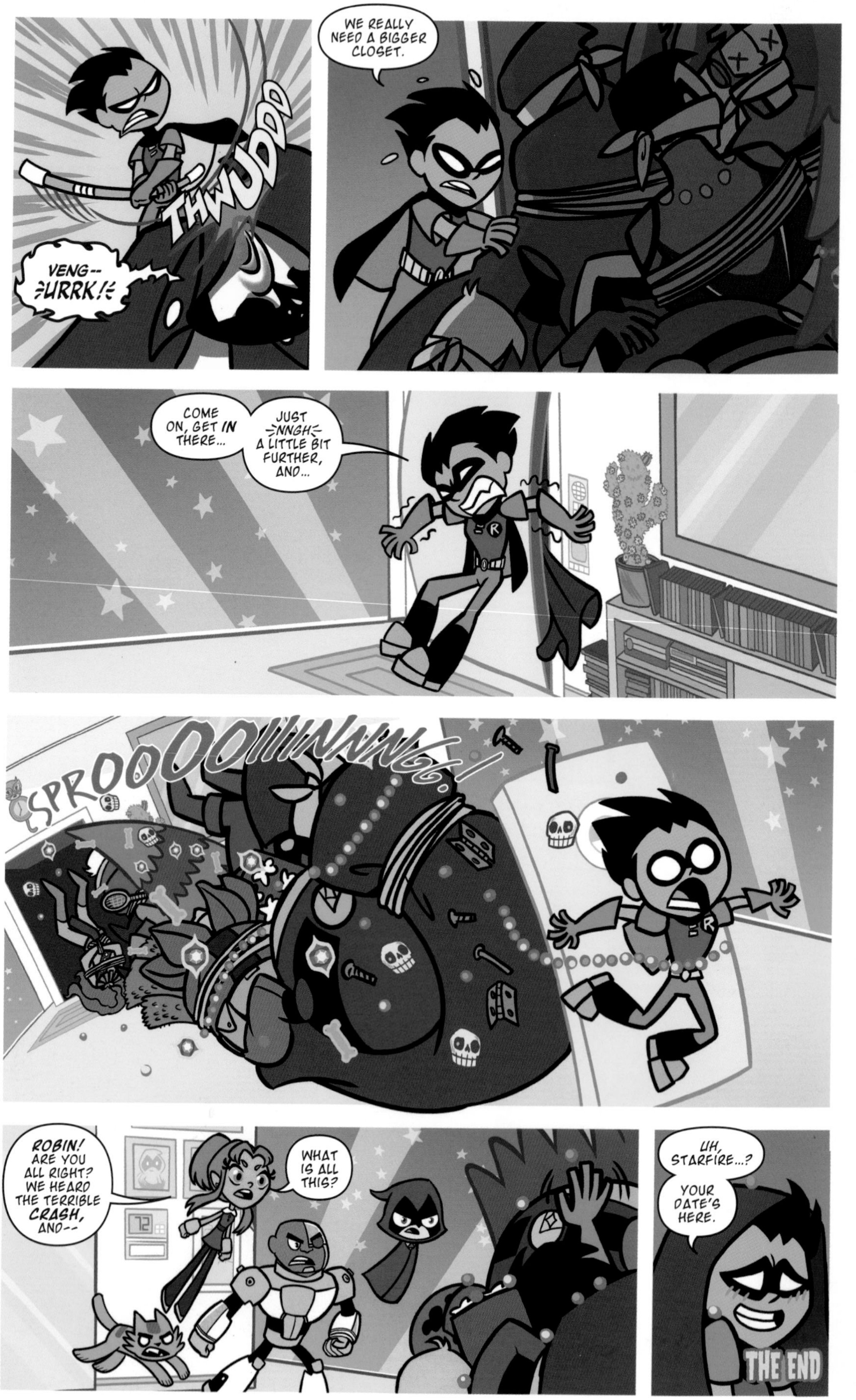
THWUDDD
VENG-- URRK!
WE REALLY NEED A BIGGER CLOSET.
COME ON, GET IN THERE...
JUST NNGH A LITTLE BIT FURTHER, AND...
SPROOOOIIIINNNGG!
ROBIN! ARE YOU ALL RIGHT? WE HEARD THE TERRIBLE CRASH, AND--
WHAT IS ALL THIS?
UH, STARFIRE...?
YOUR DATE'S HERE.
THE END

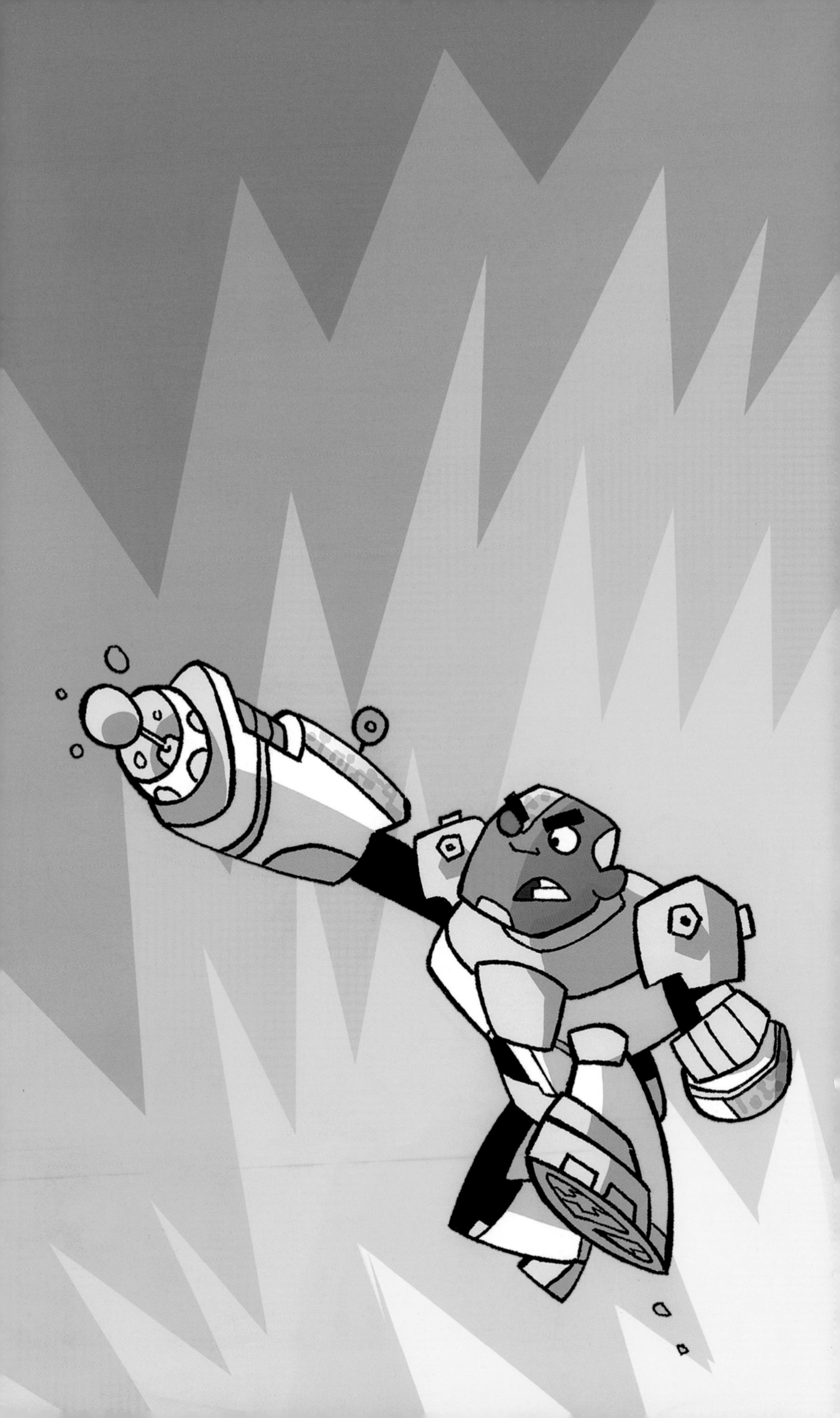

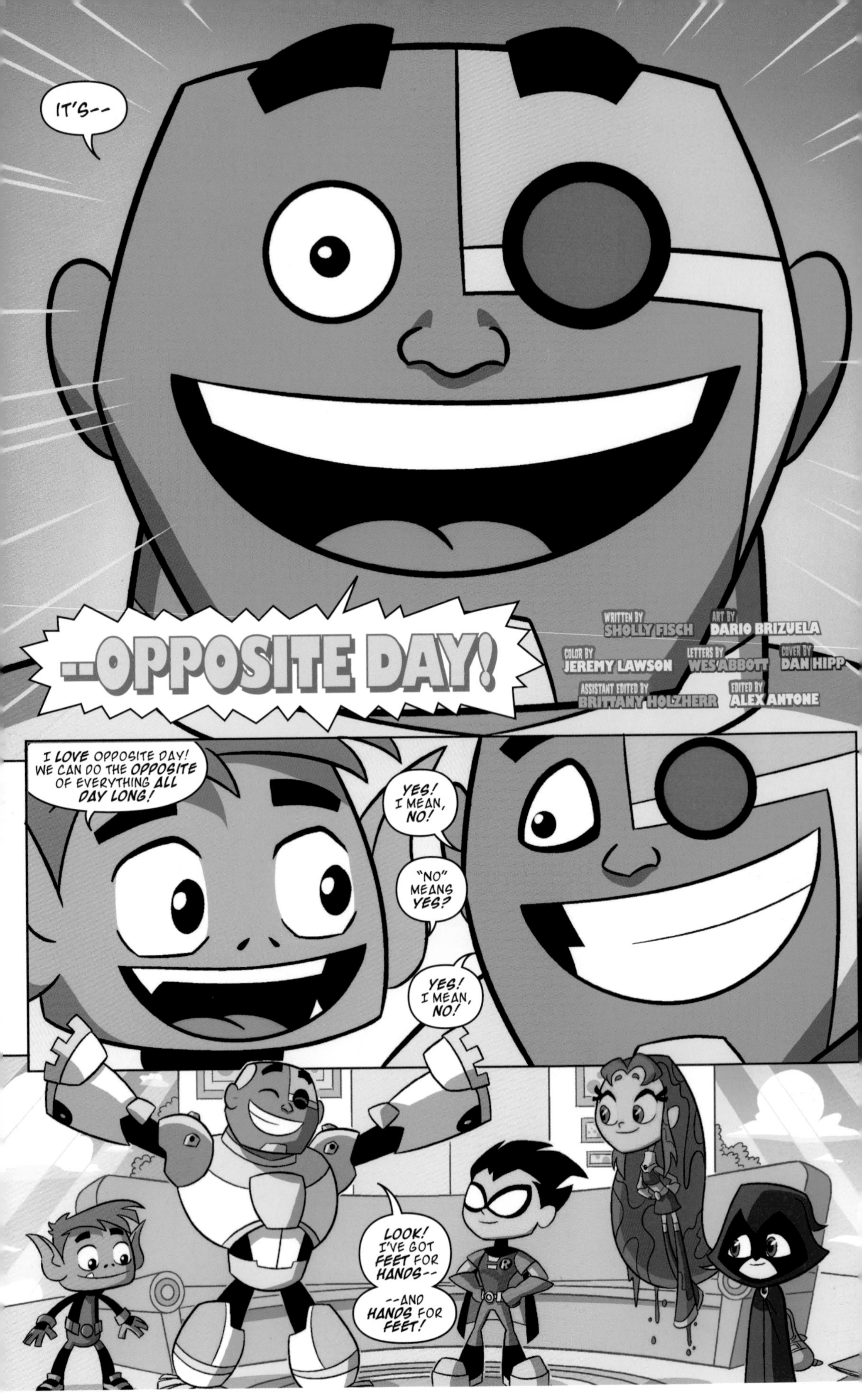
IT'S--
--OPPOSITE DAY!
WRITTEN BY SHOLLY FISCH
ART BY DARIO BRIZUELA
COLOR BY JEREMY LAWSON
LETTERS BY WES ABBOTT
COVER BY DAN HIPP
ASSISTANT EDITED BY BRITTANY HOLZHERR
EDITED BY ALEX ANTONE
I LOVE OPPOSITE DAY! WE CAN DO THE OPPOSITE OF EVERYTHING ALL DAY LONG!
YES! I MEAN, NO!
"NO" MEANS YES?
YES! I MEAN, NO!
LOOK! I'VE GOT FEET FOR HANDS--
--AND HANDS FOR FEET!

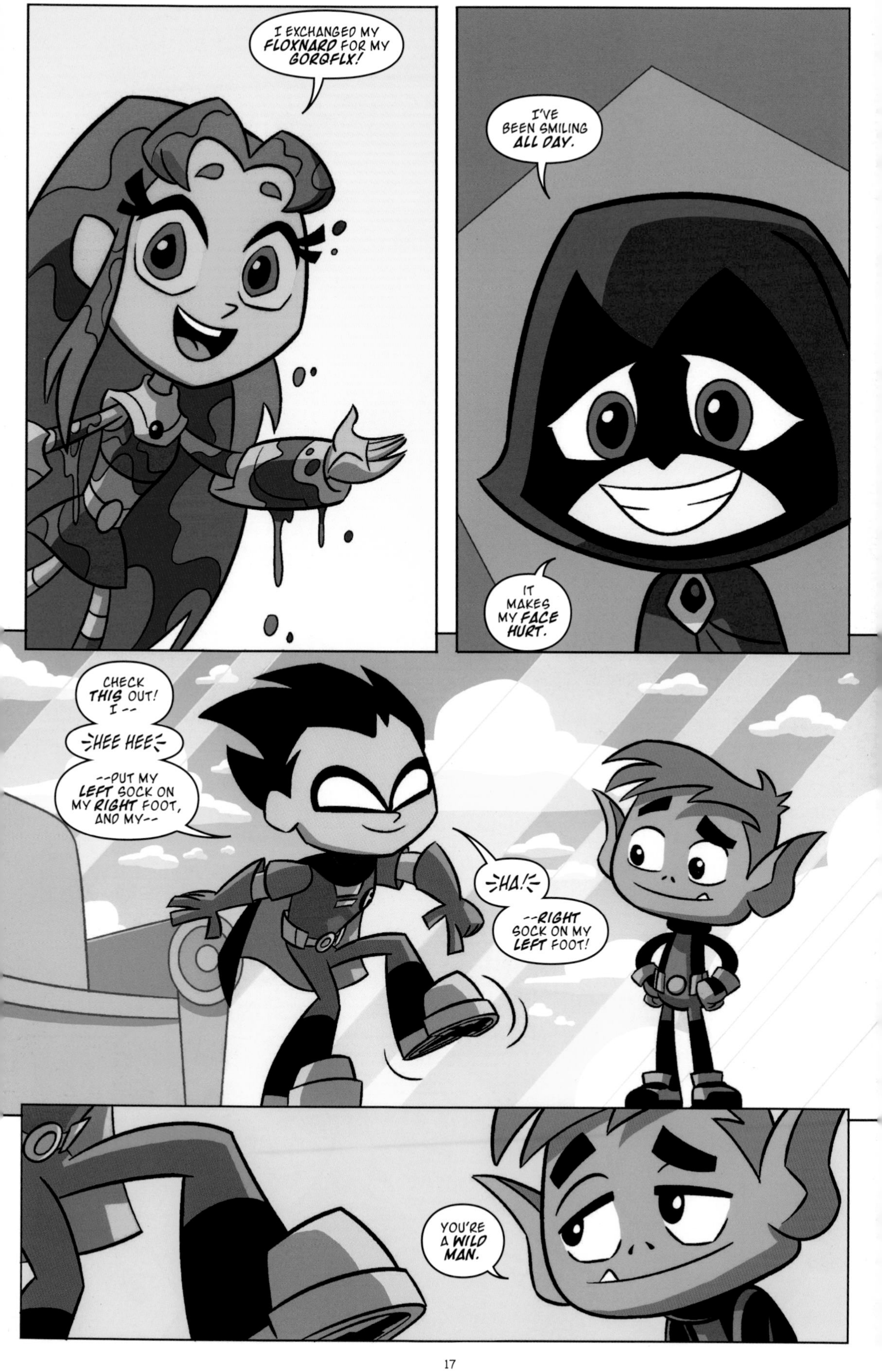
I EXCHANGED MY FLOXNARD FOR MY GORQFLX!
I'VE BEEN SMILING ALL DAY.
IT MAKES MY FACE HURT.
CHECK THIS OUT! I --
HEE HEE
--PUT MY LEFT SOCK ON MY RIGHT FOOT, AND MY--
HA!
--RIGHT SOCK ON MY LEFT FOOT!
YOU'RE A WILD MAN.

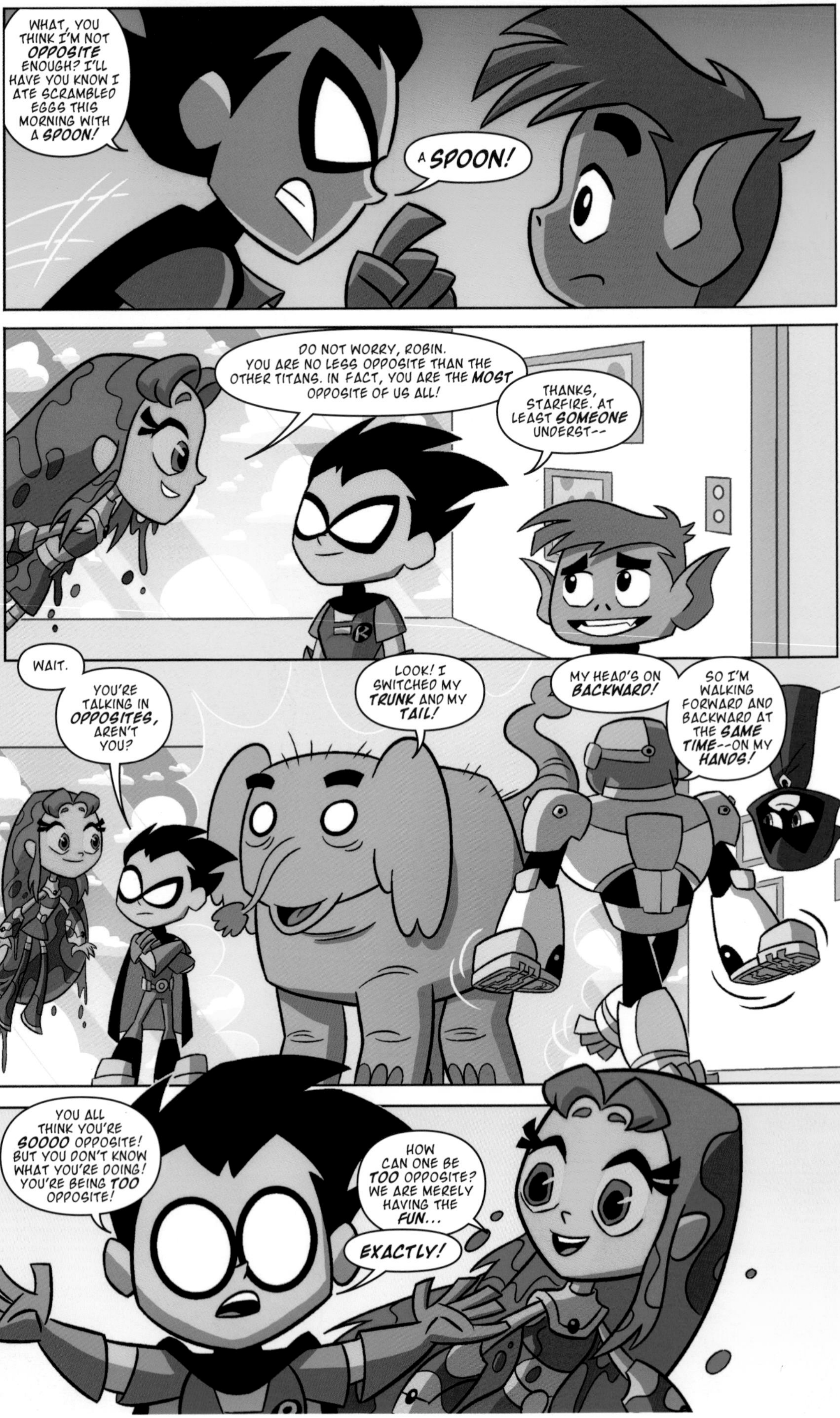

WHAT, YOU THINK I'M NOT OPPOSITE ENOUGH? I'LL HAVE YOU KNOW I ATE SCRAMBLED EGGS THIS MORNING WITH A SPOON!
A SPOON!
DO NOT WORRY, ROBIN. YOU ARE NO LESS OPPOSITE THAN THE OTHER TITANS. IN FACT, YOU ARE THE MOST OPPOSITE OF US ALL!
THANKS, STARFIRE. AT LEAST SOMEONE UNDERST--
WAIT.
YOU'RE TALKING IN OPPOSITES, AREN'T YOU?
LOOK! I SWITCHED MY TRUNK AND MY TAIL!
MY HEAD'S ON BACKWARD!
SO I'M WALKING FORWARD AND BACKWARD AT THE SAME TIME--ON MY HANDS!
YOU ALL THINK YOU'RE SOOOO OPPOSITE! BUT YOU DON'T KNOW WHAT YOU'RE DOING! YOU'RE BEING TOO OPPOSITE!
HOW CAN ONE BE TOO OPPOSITE? WE ARE MERELY HAVING THE FUN...
EXACTLY!

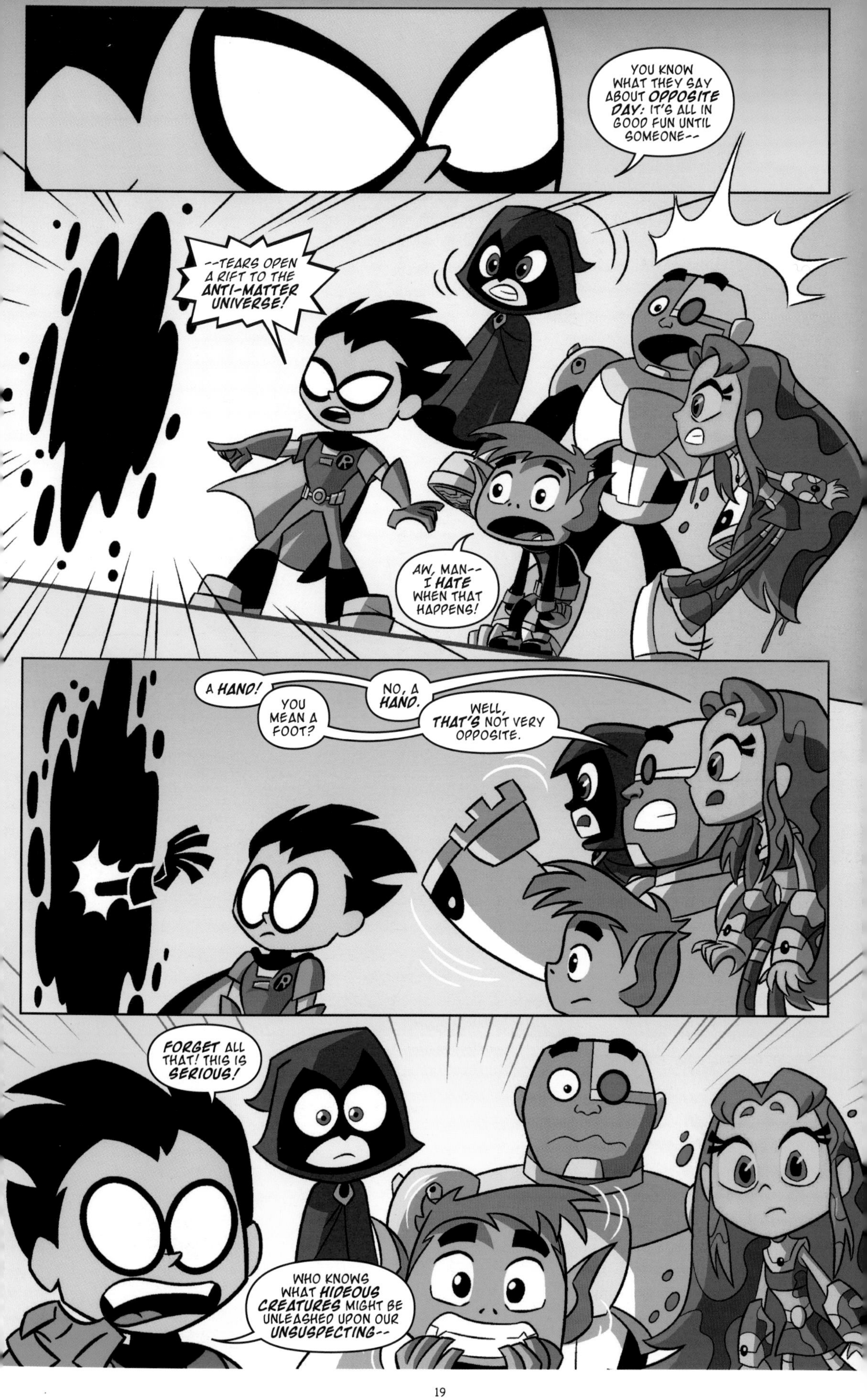
YOU KNOW WHAT THEY SAY ABOUT OPPOSITE DAY: IT'S ALL IN GOOD FUN UNTIL SOMEONE--
--TEARS OPEN A RIFT TO THE ANTI-MATTER UNIVERSE!
AW, MAN-- I HATE WHEN THAT HAPPENS!
A HAND!
YOU MEAN A FOOT?
NO, A HAND.
WELL, THAT'S NOT VERY OPPOSITE.
FORGET ALL THAT! THIS IS SERIOUS!
WHO KNOWS WHAT HIDEOUS CREATURES MIGHT BE UNLEASHED UPON OUR UNSUSPECTING--

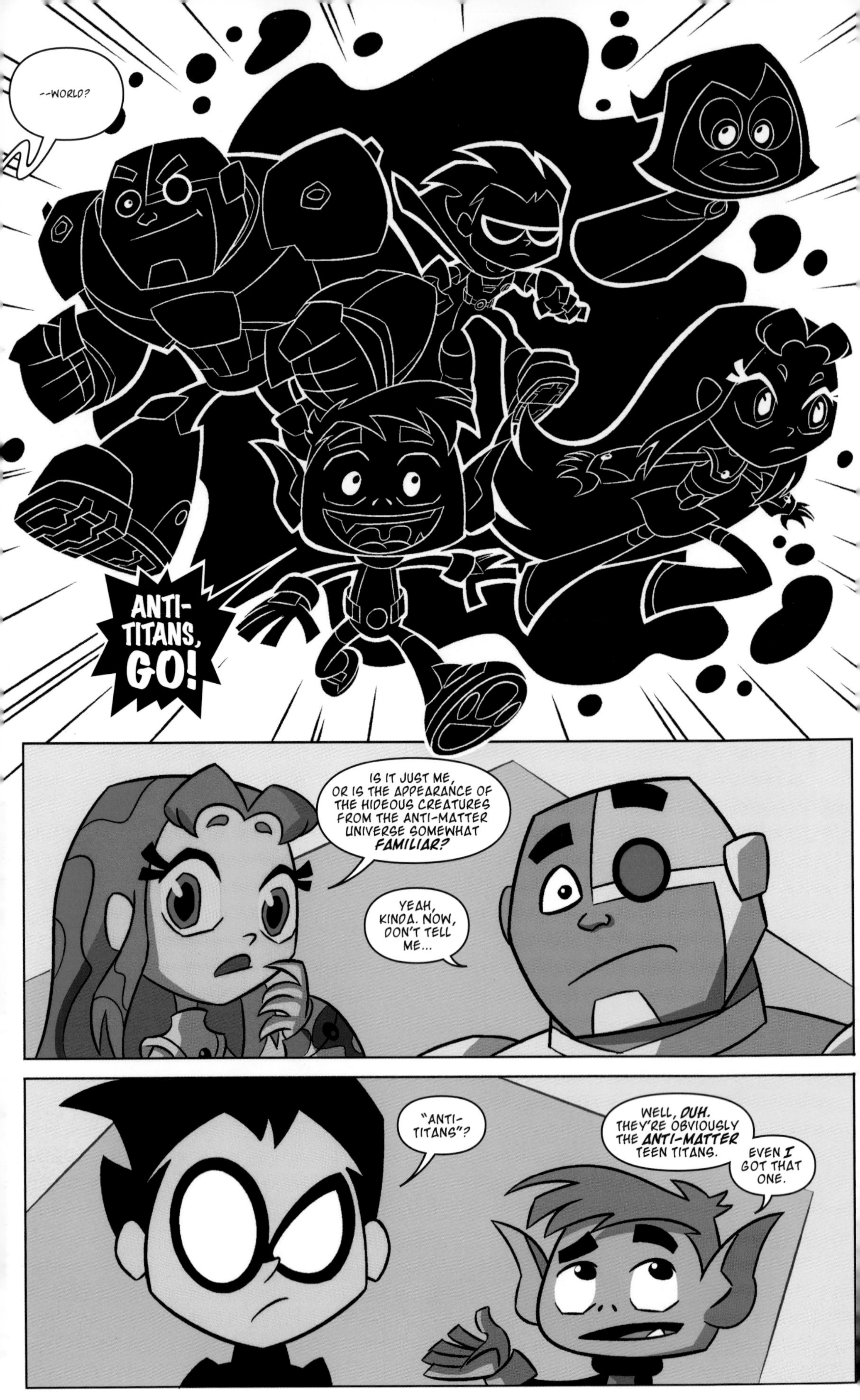
--WORLD?
ANTI-TITANS, GO!
IS IT JUST ME, OR IS THE APPEARANCE OF THE HIDEOUS CREATURES FROM THE ANTI-MATTER UNIVERSE SOMEWHAT FAMILIAR?
YEAH, KINDA. NOW, DON'T TELL ME...
"ANTI-TITANS"?
WELL, DUH. THEY'RE OBVIOUSLY THE ANTI-MATTER TEEN TITANS.
EVEN I GOT THAT ONE.

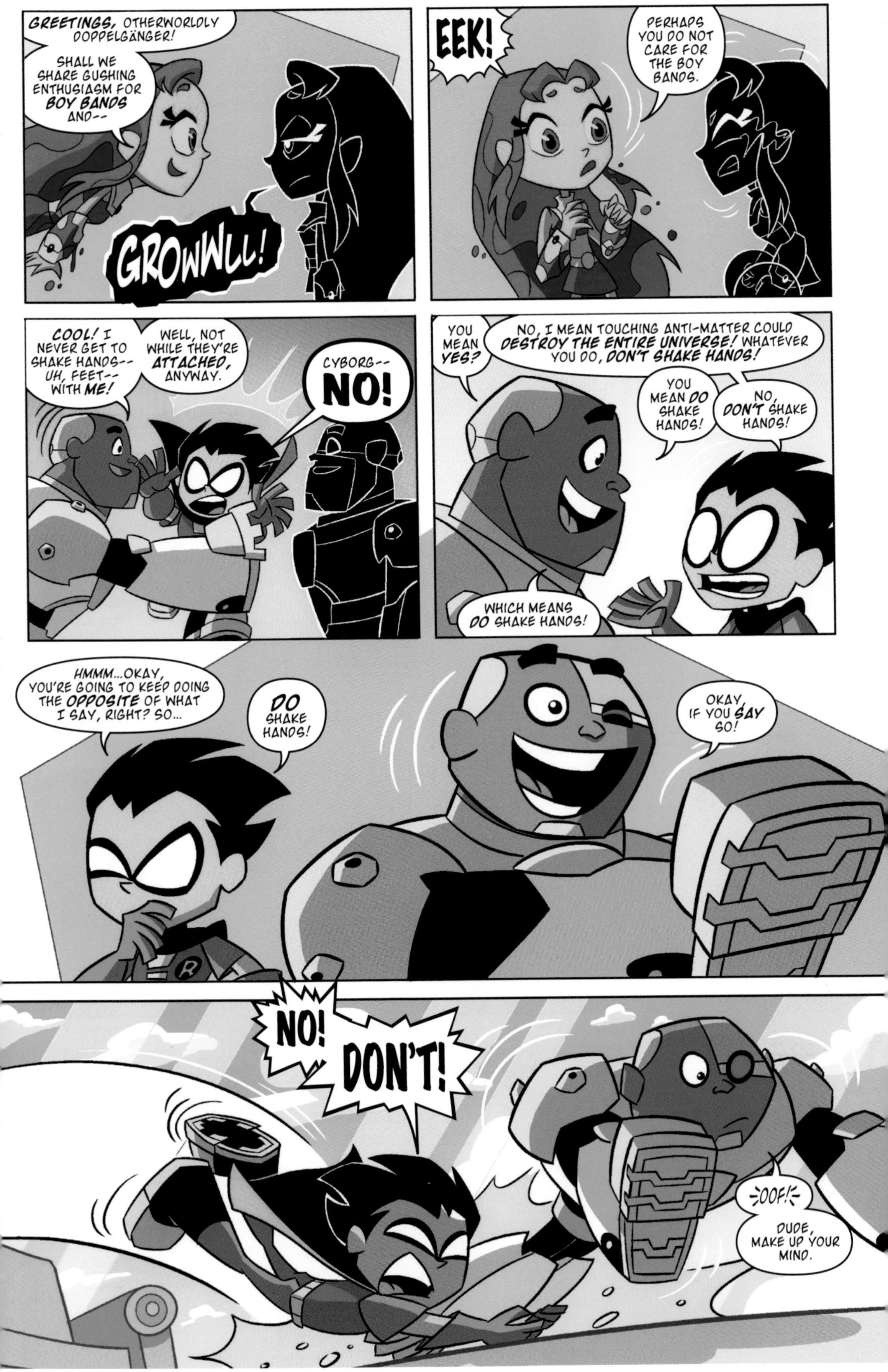
GREETINGS, OTHERWORLDLY DOPPELGÄNGER!
SHALL WE SHARE GUSHING ENTHUSIASM FOR BOY BANDS AND--
GROWWLL!
EEK!
PERHAPS YOU DO NOT CARE FOR THE BOY BANDS.
COOL! I NEVER GET TO SHAKE HANDS-- UH, FEET-- WITH ME!
WELL, NOT WHILE THEY'RE ATTACHED, ANYWAY.
CYBORG-- NO!
YOU MEAN YES?
NO, I MEAN TOUCHING ANTI-MATTER COULD DESTROY THE ENTIRE UNIVERSE! WHATEVER YOU DO, DON'T SHAKE HANDS!
YOU MEAN DO SHAKE HANDS!
NO, DON'T SHAKE HANDS!
WHICH MEANS DO SHAKE HANDS!
HMMM...OKAY, YOU'RE GOING TO KEEP DOING THE OPPOSITE OF WHAT I SAY, RIGHT? SO...
DO SHAKE HANDS!
OKAY, IF YOU SAY SO!
NO!
DON'T!
OOF!
DUDE, MAKE UP YOUR MIND.

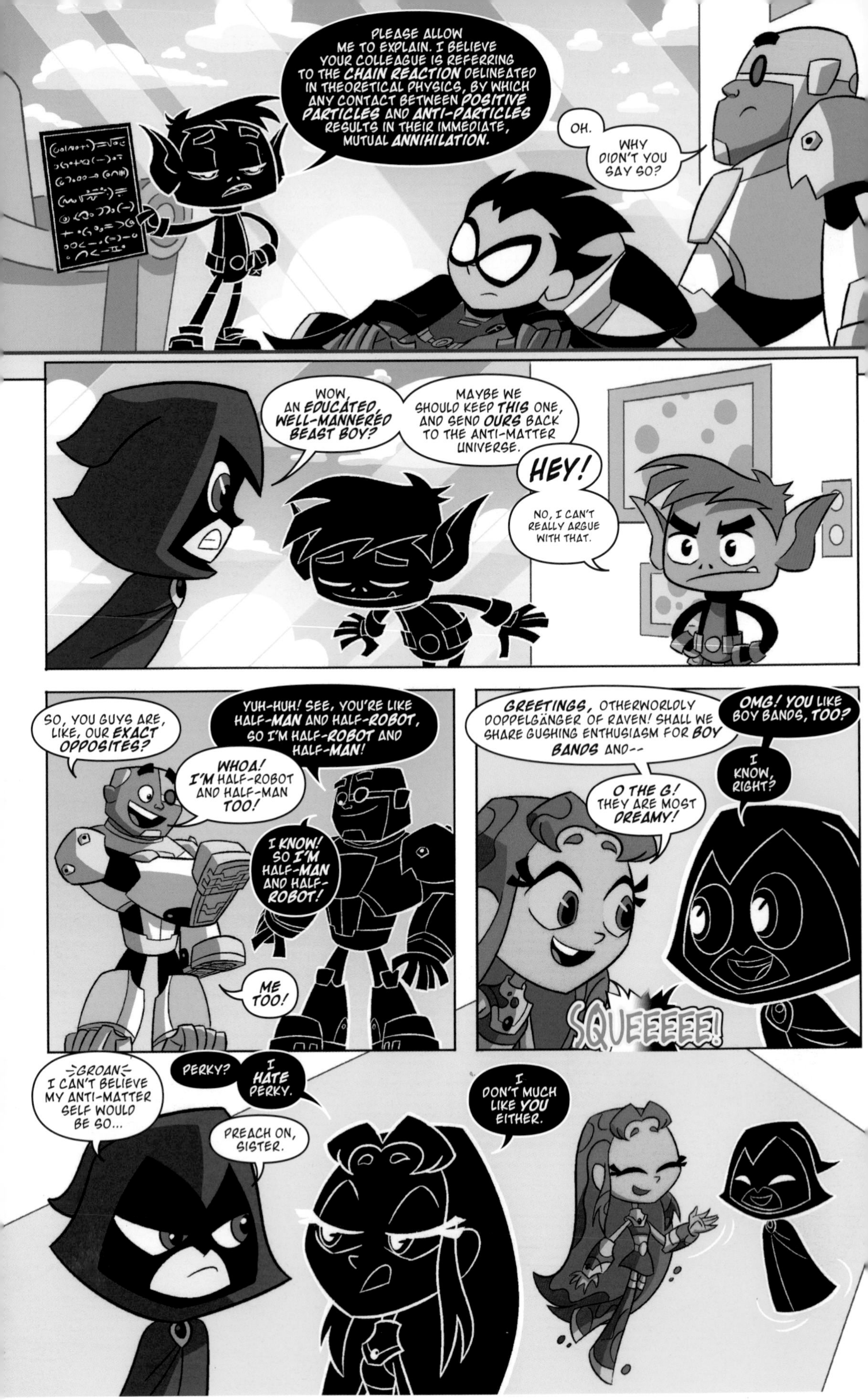

PLEASE ALLOW ME TO EXPLAIN. I BELIEVE YOUR COLLEAGUE IS REFERRING TO THE CHAIN REACTION DELINEATED IN THEORETICAL PHYSICS, BY WHICH ANY CONTACT BETWEEN POSITIVE PARTICLES AND ANTI-PARTICLES RESULTS IN THEIR IMMEDIATE, MUTUAL ANNIHILATION.
OH.
WHY DIDN'T YOU SAY SO?
WOW, AN EDUCATED, WELL-MANNERED BEAST BOY?
MAYBE WE SHOULD KEEP THIS ONE, AND SEND OURS BACK TO THE ANTI-MATTER UNIVERSE.
HEY!
NO, I CAN'T REALLY ARGUE WITH THAT.
SO, YOU GUYS ARE, LIKE, OUR EXACT OPPOSITES?
YUH-HUH! SEE, YOU'RE LIKE HALF-MAN AND HALF-ROBOT, SO I'M HALF-ROBOT AND HALF-MAN!
WHOA! I'M HALF-ROBOT AND HALF-MAN TOO!
I KNOW! SO I'M HALF-MAN AND HALF-ROBOT!
ME TOO!
GREETINGS, OTHERWORLDLY DOPPELGÄNGER OF RAVEN! SHALL WE SHARE GUSHING ENTHUSIASM FOR BOY BANDS AND--
OMG! YOU LIKE BOY BANDS, TOO?
I KNOW, RIGHT?
O THE G! THEY ARE MOST DREAMY!
SQUEEEEEE!
=GROAN= I CAN'T BELIEVE MY ANTI-MATTER SELF WOULD BE SO...
PERKY?
I HATE PERKY.
PREACH ON, SISTER.
I DON'T MUCH LIKE YOU EITHER.

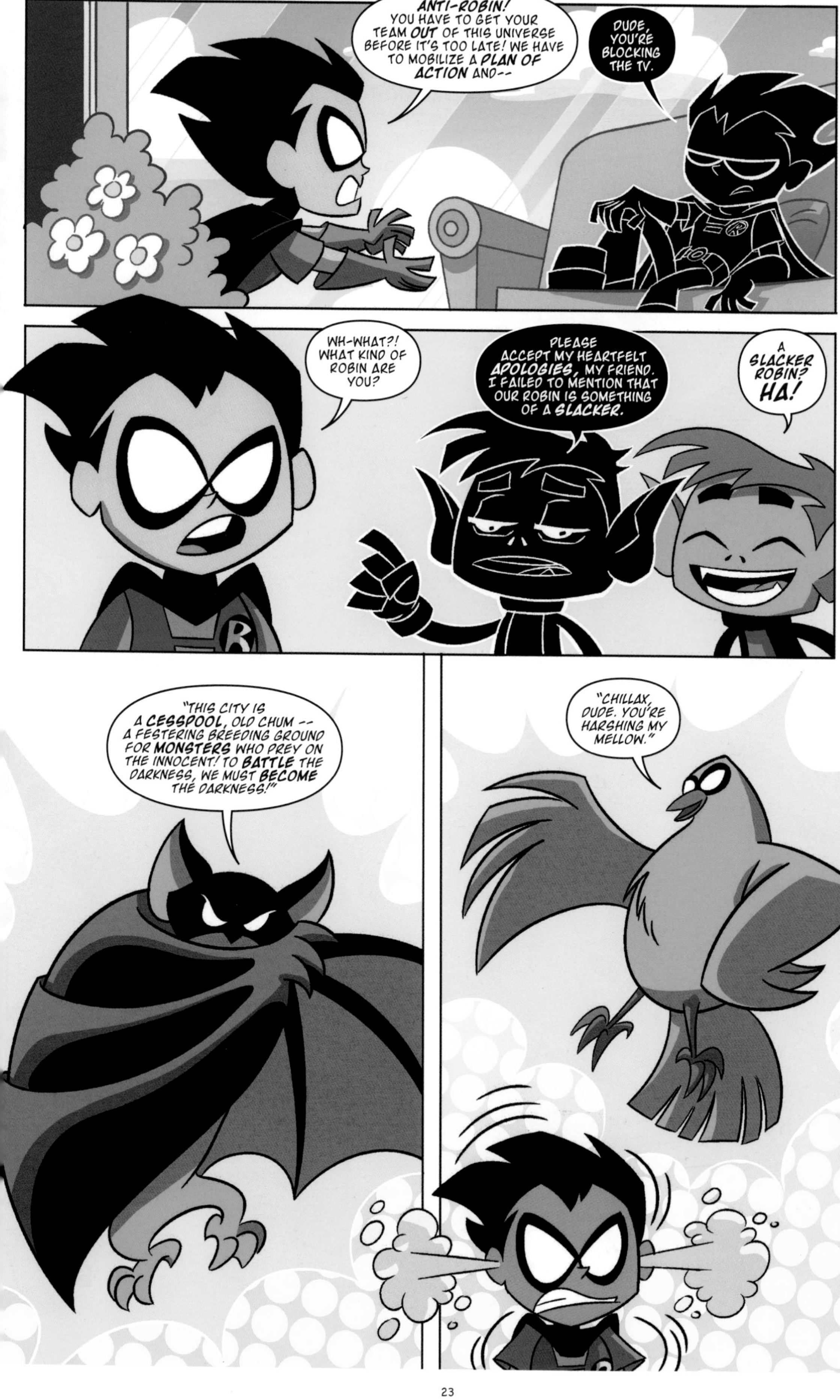

ANTI-ROBIN! YOU HAVE TO GET YOUR TEAM OUT OF THIS UNIVERSE BEFORE IT'S TOO LATE! WE HAVE TO MOBILIZE A PLAN OF ACTION AND--
DUDE, YOU'RE BLOCKING THE TV.
WH-WHAT?! WHAT KIND OF ROBIN ARE YOU?
PLEASE ACCEPT MY HEARTFELT APOLOGIES, MY FRIEND. I FAILED TO MENTION THAT OUR ROBIN IS SOMETHING OF A SLACKER.
A SLACKER ROBIN? HA!
"THIS CITY IS A CESSPOOL, OLD CHUM -- A FESTERING BREEDING GROUND FOR MONSTERS WHO PREY ON THE INNOCENT! TO BATTLE THE DARKNESS, WE MUST BECOME THE DARKNESS!"
"CHILLAX, DUDE. YOU'RE HARSHING MY MELLOW."

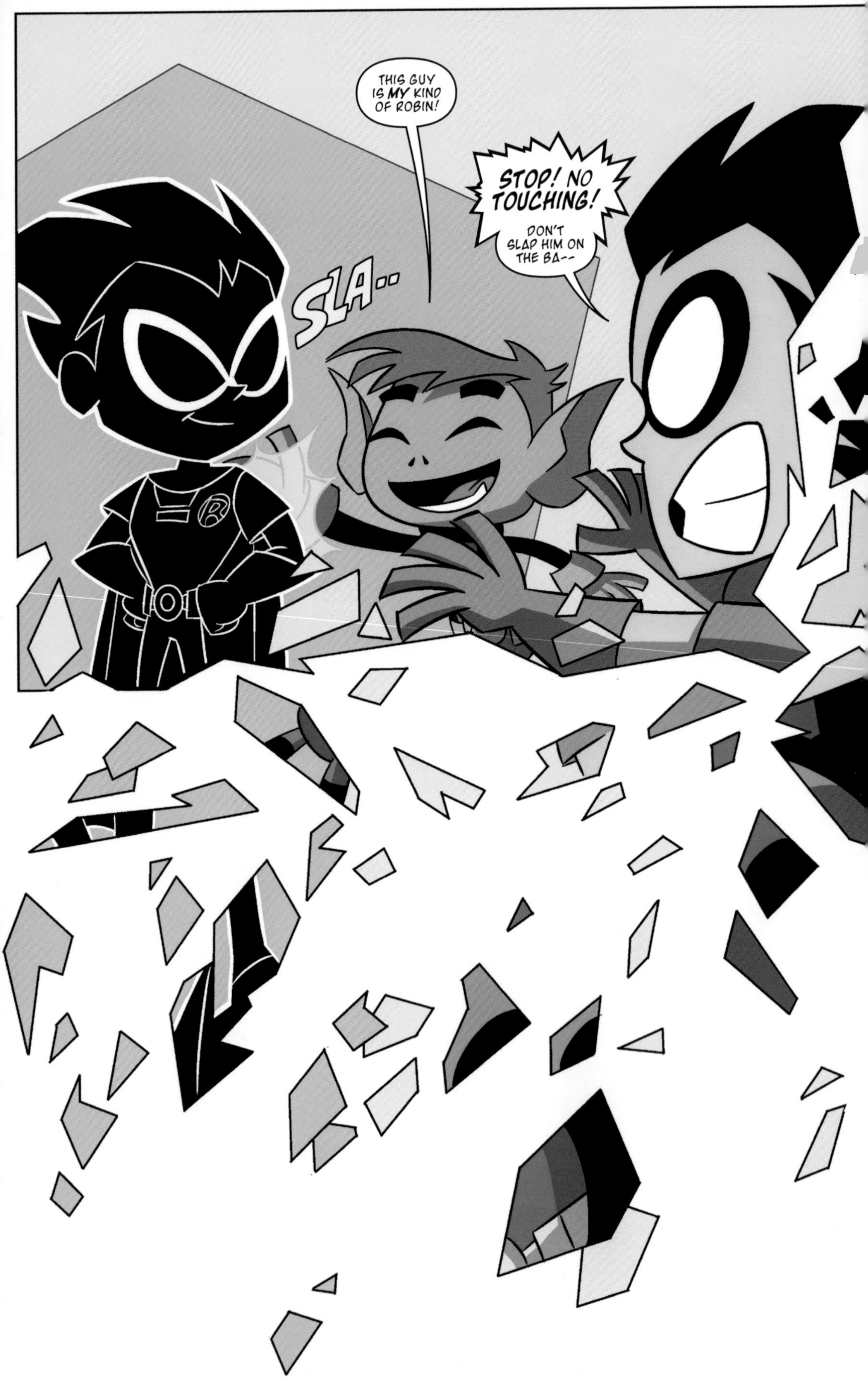
THIS GUY IS MY KIND OF ROBIN!
STOP! NO TOUCHING!
DON'T SLAP HIM ON THE BA--
SLA..

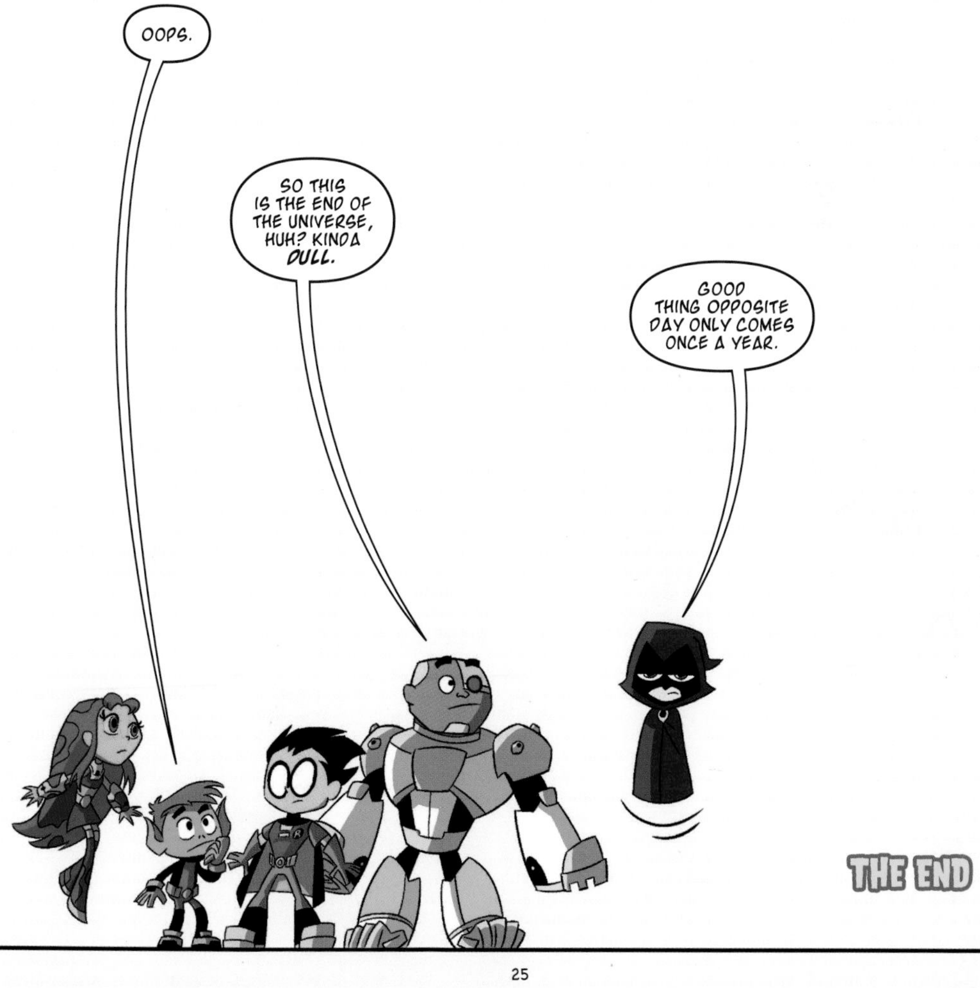
OOPS.
SO THIS IS THE END OF THE UNIVERSE, HUH? KINDA DULL.
GOOD THING OPPOSITE DAY ONLY COMES ONCE A YEAR.
THE END

CREATORS

SHOLLY FISCH

Bitten by a radioactive typewriter, Sholly Fisch has spent the wee hours writing books, comics, TV scripts, and online material for over 25 years. His comic book credits include more than 200 stories and features about characters such as Batman, Superman, Bugs Bunny, Daffy Duck, Spider-Man, and Ben 10. Currently, he writes stories for Action Comics every month, plus stories for Looney Tunes and Scooby-Doo. By day, Sholly is a mild-mannered developmental psychologist who helps to create educational TV shows, websites, and other media for kids.

LEA HERNANDEZ

Lea Hernandez is a comic book artist and webcomic creator who is known for her manga-influenced style. She has worked with Marvel Comics, Oni Press, NBM Publishing, and DC Comics. In addition to her work on Teen Titans Go!, she is the co-creator of Killer Princesses and the creator of Rumble Girls.

DARIO BRIZUELA

Dario Brizuela was born in Buenos Aires, Argentina, in 1977. He enjoys doing illustration work and character design for several companies including DC Comics, Marvel Comics, Image Comics, IDW Publishing, Titan Publishing, Hasbro, Capstone Publishers, and Disney Publishing Worldwide. Dario's work can be found in a wide range of properties including Star Wars Tales, Ben 10, DC Super Friends, Justice League Unlimited, Batman: The Brave & The Bold, Transformers, Teenage Mutant Ninja Turtles, Batman 66, Wonder Woman 77, Teen Titans Go!, Scooby-Doo! Team Up, and DC Super Hero Girls.

GLOSSARY

annihilation (uh-nye-uh-LAY-shuhn)—the state of being completely destroyed

anti-matter (AN-tee-mat-er)—matter whose parts match parts of ordinary matter except in having some opposite properties (as a positive instead of a negative charge)

cesspool (SESS-pool)—a pit in the ground that holds human waste and other garbage

debase (dih-BAYS)—to lower the value of something or someone

delineate (dih-LIN-ee-ayt)—to clearly show or describe

doppelgänger (DOP-uhl-gang-er)—someone who looks like someone else

embark (em-BAHRK)—to start something that is new

humiliate (hyoo-MIL-ee-ate)—to make someone look or feel foolish or embarrassed

hunchback (HUHNCH-bak)—a person with a humped or crooked back

miscreant (MIS-kree-uhnt)—a villain

mobilize (MOH-buh-lize)—to come together for action

obligate (OB-li-gayt)—to make someone do something because it is right or because the law requires it

otherworldly (uhth-er-WURLD-lee)—seeming to come from another world

perky (PUR-kee)—cheerful

primp (PRIMP)—to groom oneself carefully

shapeshift (SHAYP-shift)—to change form or identity

slacker (SLAK-er)—a person who avoids work

suitor (SOO-tur)—a man who is courting a woman

unleash (uhn-LEESH)—to cause or allow something very powerful to happen

uphold (up-HOHLD)—to support something

VISUAL QUESTIONS & WRITING PROMPTS

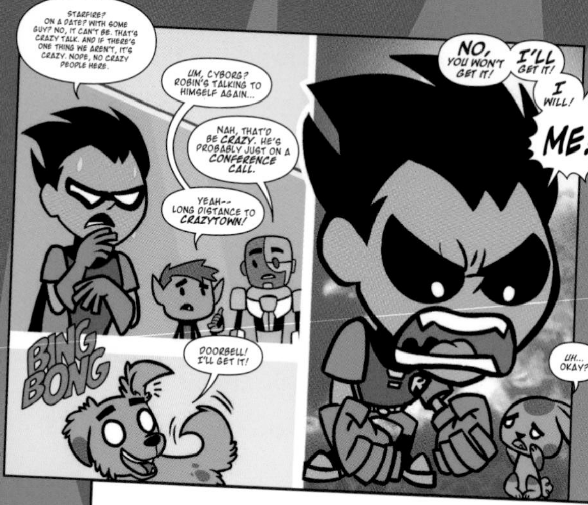
STARFIRE? ON A DATE? WITH SOME GUY? NO, IT CAN'T BE. THAT'S CRAZY TALK. AND IF THERE'S ONE THING WE AREN'T, IT'S CRAZY. NOPE, NO CRAZY PEOPLE HERE.
UM, CYBORG? ROBIN'S TALKING TO HIMSELF AGAIN...
NAH, THAT'D BE CRAZY. HE'S PROBABLY JUST ON A CONFERENCE CALL.
YEAH-- LONG DISTANCE TO CRAZYTOWN!
BING BONG
DOORBELL! I'LL GET IT!
NO, YOU WON'T GET IT!
I'LL GET IT!
I WILL!
ME!
UH... OKAY?

1. How do you think Robin feels about Starfire going on dates? What clues in the text and art make you think this?

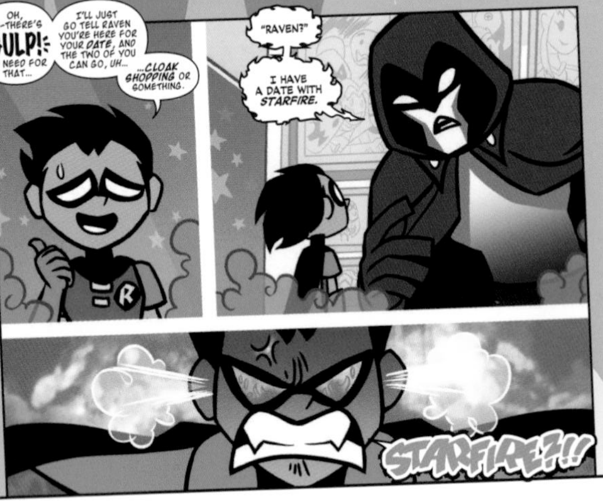
OH, TH-THERE'S GULP! NO NEED FOR THAT...
I'LL JUST GO TELL RAVEN YOU'RE HERE FOR YOUR DATE, AND THE TWO OF YOU CAN GO, UH...
...CLOAK SHOPPING OR SOMETHING.
"RAVEN?"
I HAVE A DATE WITH STARFIRE.
STARFIRE?!!

2. When the Spectre shows up, Robin assumes he's there to meet Raven. How does his reaction change when he learns that the Spectre is actually there for Starfire?

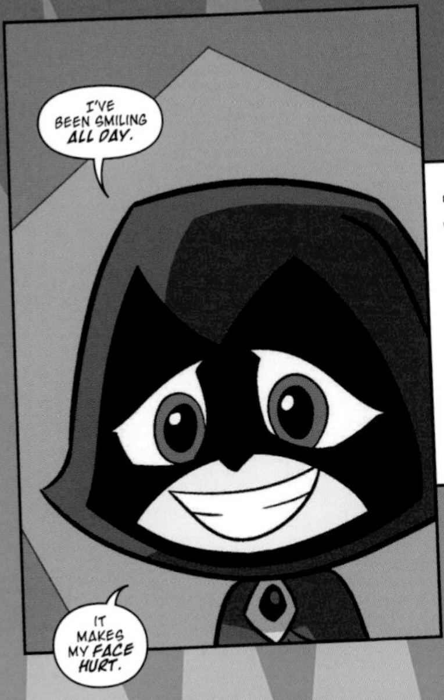

I'VE BEEN SMILING ALL DAY.
IT MAKES MY FACE HURT.

3. Raven celebrates Opposite Day by smiling all day long. How do the other Titans show it's Opposite Day? Turn to pages 16 and 17 for help.

4. What clues do the creators give you that the Anti-Titans are different from the Titans? Give some examples.

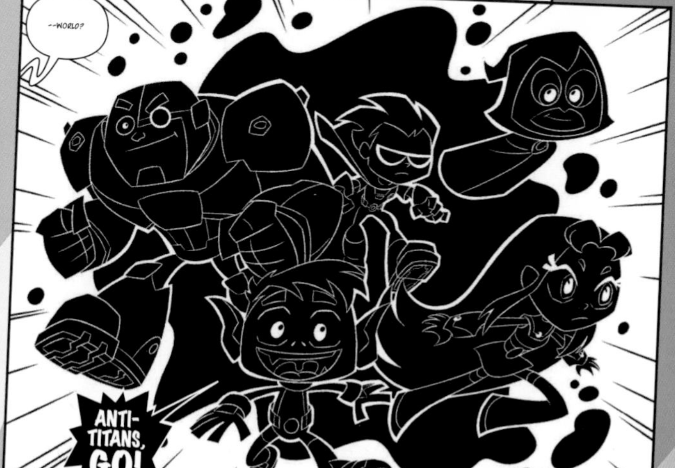

--WORLD?
ANTI-TITANS, GO!

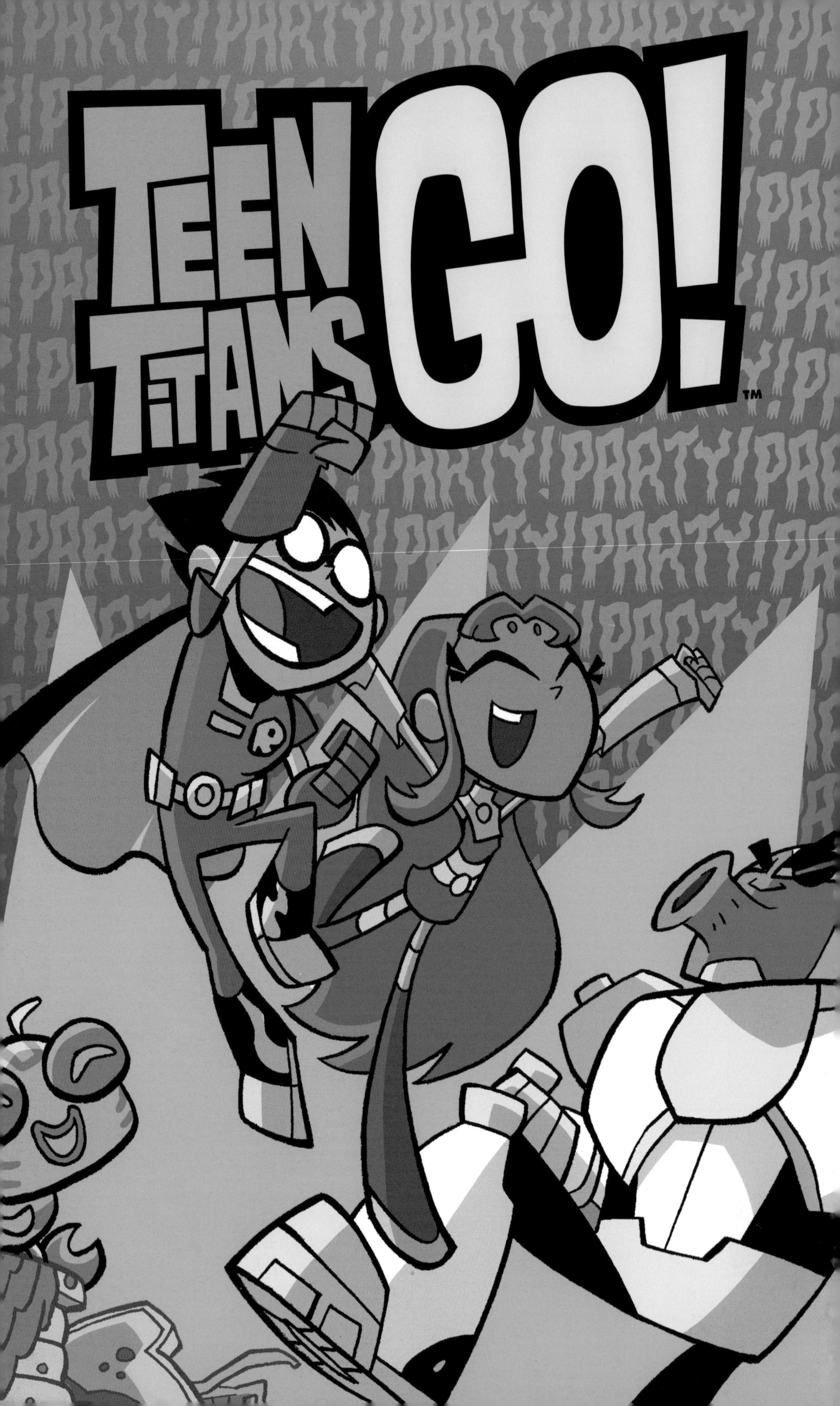

TEEN TITANS GO!

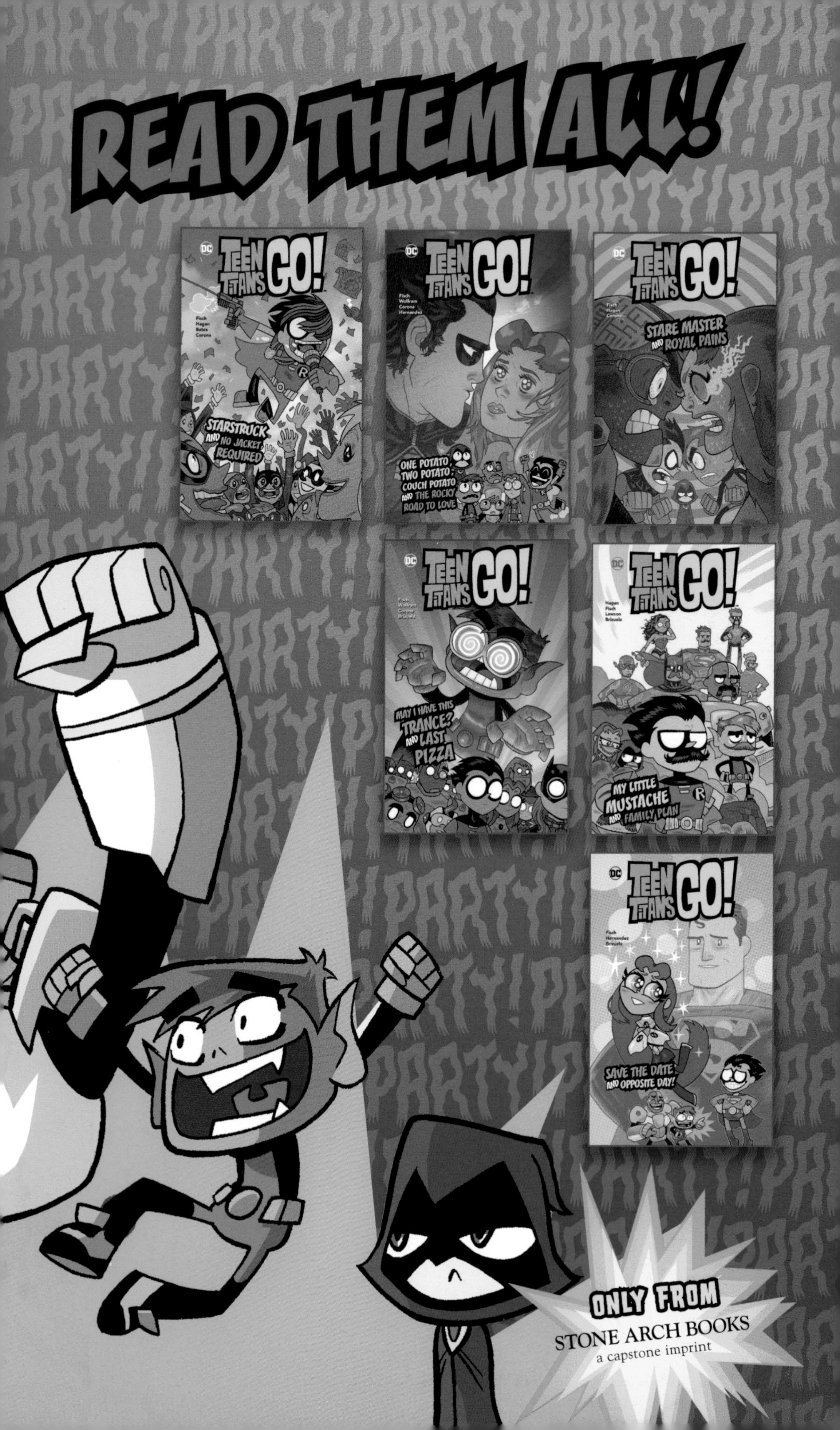

READ THEM ALL!
TEEN TITANS GO!
STARSTRUCK AND NO JACKET REQUIRED
TEEN TITANS GO!
ONE POTATO, TWO POTATO, COUCH POTATO AND THE ROCKY ROAD TO LOVE
TEEN TITANS GO!
STARE MASTER AND ROYAL PAINS
TEEN TITANS GO!
MAY I HAVE THIS TRANCE? AND LAST PIZZA
TEEN TITANS GO!
MY LITTLE MUSTACHE AND FAMILY PLAN
TEEN TITANS GO!
SAVE THE DATE AND OPPOSITE DAY!
ONLY FROM
STONE ARCH BOOKS
a capstone imprint

TEEN TITANS GO!™